"We have matters to discuss before we leave London," Nikolai told Lucy, his voice deep and pleasant though it was, jarring her already overstrung nerves. She was well on the way to disliking this new cousin, and they had not yet spent half an hour in each other's company. She looked up, intending to respond, but her words were forgotten as Nikolai moved fractionally and the light from the windows fell sharply on his face highlighting the long white scar that ran from his temple to his jaw.

"Unpleasant, isn't it?" His tanned fingers traced the thin line. "A legacy from a duel fought before the Tsar forbade them. We Russians are a people whose blood runs hot, Lucy Stanton. And you, whose blood has been thinned by the cautious Englishness of your father, would do well to remember that. You will grow accustomed to it, as I have. Now, let us return to the arrangements for our journey."

He had dismissed the scar lightly, but Lucy sensed that behind the cold demeanor, her cousin was deeply sensitive about it. She stole a glance at the aloof profile. A duel he had said. Over what? A woman? Surely not. A matter of honor more likely. He was a man who would hold his honor very dear indeed . . .

Novels By Caroline Courtney

Duchess in Disguise
A Wager For Love
Love Unmasked
The Fortunes of Love
Guardian of the Heart
Dangerous Engagement
Love's Masquerade
Love Triumphant
Heart of Honor
Libertine in Love
The Romantic Rivals
Forbidden Love
Abandoned For Love
The Tempestuous Affair

Published By
WARNER BOOKS

CAROLINE COURTNEY

The Tempestuous Affair

WARNER BOOKS

A Warner Communications Company

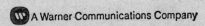

The
Tempestuous
Affair

One

Stanton Lacey had been the home of the Stantons since the time of William the Conqueror. Twenty-odd generations of Stanton males had inherited the estate in a direct, unbroken line; twenty-odd generations of Stanton wives had dutifully presented their spouses with a male heir.

But now, for the first time since the days of the Norman Baron de Stauntanne, who had been granted the lands for his services to William, Stanton Lacey was moving outside the family. The house was passing to a third cousin of no particular account; a mere baronet with nothing to recommend him save for the fact that his family had become prominent during the turbulent days of Henry VIII's reign, and had intermarried with the Stantons, thus giving him the right to claim Stanton Lacey for his own in the absence of a direct male heir.

Miss Lucy Stanton had taken refuge in the nursery, driven thence by the vociferous protests of the "aunts" who had gathered in the drawing room, supposedly to mourn the passing of her dearest papa, but in reality to decimate without mercy, the character, person, and manners of the new owner of Stanton Lacey.

The "aunts" were a cross Lucy had inherited from her father, because, in reality, they were *his* aunts, rather than hers. However, the twenty-year gap between the arrival of Lucy's grandfather and the birth of his eldest sister had meant that these ladies were nearer in age to their nephew than their brother; a fact which Sir Charles Stanton had never ceased to regret since they adopted toward him the bossy, dictatorial manner of "elder sisters."

During his life-time he had done what he could to shield his own daughter from the aunt's sharp tongues, but he had not been able to stop them from habitually criticizing everything about her from her looks to the way he had brought her up.

When they had learned that Sir Charles intended to teach Lucy himself they had thrown up their hands in horror. She would turn out to be a bookish "bluestocking" they declared ominously. As for learning French, why it was positively unpatriotic, with that parvenu Bonaparte setting himself up as emperor and the French aristocracy starving in London slums. Worse was to follow when they discovered that Sir Charles had been educating his daughter in Politics! Educating females could only lead to TROUBLE Aunt Maria had declared portentously, and Charles was a fool for trying.

And their criticisms did not stop there. No Stanton had ever had hair that particular shade of blue black, nor eyes the color of mountain gentians, fringed with lashes so long and thick they looked positively unreal. And as for Lucy's temperament! No Stanton female had ever possessed such a perverse streak of wilful disobedience; Stanton women were always meek, biddable creatures, whose looks never drove a man to anything but passive indifference.

Following her father's advice, Lucy had tried her best to ignore the aunt's criticisms. They sprang from jealousy, Sir Charles explained. Jealousy, not only of the vivacious beauty of the girl he had made his wife, but also of the fact that because she was a Russian Princess in her own right, Lucy's Mama took precedence over her husband's aunts. It was all very well for Aunt Maria to sniff disparagingly that all the world knew that foreign titles were ten a penny and that she preferred a good old-fashioned English baronet any day, but that did not alter the fact that in sociey their niece-in-law ranked ahead of them. None of them had made the slightest attempt to welcome the new bride to England, rather the opposite, and as had been proved at the reading of his Will, Sir Charles had neither forgotten nor forgiven their slighting snubs.

Lucy had never known her mother and had to rely on her papa for stories of that gay, laughing girl whose face smiled down at her from the portrait above the fire in papa's study.

Her parents had met when Sir Charles was visiting Russia. The English Ambassador had introduced them at a ball and Sir Charles, newly come into the title, fell instantly and irrevocably in love with the beautiful Russian girl.

It was only later that he learned that the ball had been given to mark the Princess Nadia's betrothal to the man her parents had chosen for her when she was still in the cradle; but by then it was too late, for Nadia was as much in love with the handsome Englishman as he was with her.

Sir Charles had been adamant at first that he would not marry Nadia without her father's permission. Manfully he had hardened his heart against her tears when she pleaded with him not to approach her parents. He came of a good family and had a respectable fortune, and could hardly comprehend the violent storm of abuse Nadia's father unleashed upon him when he called to see him to plead his case. Scornfully the old Prince told him of the vast estates owned by the man he had chosen for his daughter's husband; his close connections with the Tsar; his ancestry so closely aligned to Nadia's own. Did he seriously believe that any father would allow a daughter to throw herself away on so worthless a match as Sir Charles proposed when such a marriage had been arranged? Stumblingly Sir Charles had told him of his love, but the old Prince refused to listen, threatening to have his serfs horsewhip him out of St. Petersburg if he tried to contact Nadia again.

It had been this last insult that lit the fuse of Sir Charles's own anger. That very night he had gone secretly to Nadia and told her what had transpired. She never hesitated, and by morning they were married by an English clergyman living in St. Petersburg. Then with the surreptitious help of friends the newly married pair made their way to England.

Her family had never forgiven her. Sir Charles himself had written to them on the birth of Lucy, but received no reply. A year later he had the sad task of writing once more, this time to tell them of Nadia's tragic death in childbirth. The letter was never acknowledged. Already suffering deeply over the death of his beloved wife, bitter hatred for her family entered Sir Charles's soul, and he made a vow that from thence onward his wife's family would cease to exist.

The aunts were delighted. Always envious of Nadia they saw this as a sign that their nephew was beginning to regret his impulsive marriage. Nothing could have been further from the truth, and to prove it Sir Charles steadfastly refused to listen to the blandishments and pleas of his relatives to take a second wife and provide himself with an heir.

Lucy and her father had been very close. Even now she could not believe that he was dead; that she would never again hear his beloved voice or see his dear face. A tear trickled down her face, mingling with the dust on the window seat. The nursery had been closed up for years, but today she had felt a need for its secure familiarity. A sob rose and was choked back. It would never do for the aunts to see her like this.

Aunt Maria was the worst—Aunt Maria who was married to an earl and had been used to considering herself something of a personage until her nephew had brought home his Russian bride. She had never forgiven Nadia for usurping her position as First Lady of the Stanton family, and during the all too brief time of Nadia's marriage had gone out of her way to make things difficult for the new bride.

Since she was the eldest, the others nearly always followed dutifully where Aunt Maria led. Only Aunt Phoebe, the spinster member of the quartet had made a few, tentative efforts to make the stranger feel welcome but these were soon quelled by her elder sisters.

Jessica, the third sister, married to a baronet and the mother of three daughters, had been scornful of Phoebe's bumbling attempts to pour oil on troubled waters. "Romantic!" she had said derisively. "How foolish you are, sister, romance has nothing to do with marriage!" Aunt Jessica believed in sensible, arranged matches between persons of equal birth and fortune. Marriages like those she had contracted for her own daughters.

Lucy had suffered by comparison to Aunt Jessica's daughters all her life. According to their Mama, they were perfect paragons of female behavior. *They* had all had the benefit of a correct upbringing. They could all execute tasteful, insipid water colors; play the pianoforte, and make genteel small talk with any gentleman fortunate enough to find himself in their company. Even had they known how to do so, it would never have entered their heads to engage a member of the opposite sex in a discussion about anything deeper than mere trivia; gentlemen did not care for females who could discuss the latest developments in Bonaparte's invasion of Europe, or the newest methods of husbandry and tenantry; or so their mama had taught them.

Sir Charles had thought differently. He could see no reason why Lucy should not make full use of the excellent brain she possessed and frequently told his relatives so. But now there was no papa to stand between Lucy and the aunts's disapproval. And disapprove they did. Lucy only had to remember their reaction to papa's Will to realize how much.

"What's done is done." Aunt Jane had said briskly when the lawyer had left them. "For myself I cannot think why Charles did not tell us what he intended instead of leaving us to discover it in this scrambling fashion. I should have thought one of us far better suited to take charge of Lucy than a complete stranger . . ."

"But he is her grandfather." Aunt Phoebe had interrupted timidly.

"A grandfather who made not the slightest attempt to interest himself in her until a mere two years ago." Aunt Jessica pointed out sourly. "One could almost suppose he knew of Charles's illness and Lucy's expectations ... you may depend on it that he knows the extent of her fortune to the exact penny ..."

Lucy had been unable to bear any more and had run from the room, trying to stem her tears. She was still trying to come to terms with the shock of her father's Will. It had all been there in the letter the lawyer had read to them. It told of the unexpected approach from Prince Kuragin two Christmases ago, who, in his old age, regretted the gulf between himself and his daughter's child. Although the Prince's treatment of Nadia still pained Sir Charles deeply, he knew that his health was failing and had dwelt upon the letter, making plans which he kept secret from everyone but his lawyer.

Ill, burdened with the care of a headstrong, passionate young girl, Sir Charles's thoughts turned to what would become of Lucy after his death. It was then that he had made the decision which had shocked and stunned his family, Lucy included. He had taken up his pen and written to Lucy's grandfather, breaking the silence of eighteen years. Should anything happen to him while Lucy was still under-age or unmarried, she was to go to Russia and be brought up under Prince Kuragin's guardianship.

Lucy stared blindly out of the nursery window. If only he had told her of his plans. But he had known her so well. She would have protested passionately that nothing would happen to him, that she would not *let* it ... Papa had loved her very dearly and would never have done anything he thought might bring her pain. She tried to visualize herself living with one of the aunts and repressed a small shudder .... no! However strange and unfamiliar Russia might be it could not be worse than that! This thought served to lighten her gloom a little. Whatever happened she must remember that papa had done his best for her ... she sighed a little. The aunts did not share her faith. No doubt they were still discussing their nephew's shortcomings.

Sir Charles had made it plain in his Will that Prince Kuragin was more than ready to welcome his unknown granddaughter into his home. He had also pointed out that Lucy was, after all, half Russian and that it was time she learned about that part of her heritage which he had purposely prepared her for. Her French lessons; their discussions about politics . . . fresh tears welled and dripped onto the windowsill. Dearest papa, how she would miss him!

Would her grandfather seek to criticize him to her as the aunts criticized mama? Lucy's head lifted proudly. She would not let him! Her grandfather only wanted her because of her fortune, or so the aunts said, but she could not believe that. For her mama's father was extremely wealthy, papa had told her so. She had always known that one day she would inherit a considerable fortune. Stanton Lacey was entailed to the next male in line, but the Stanton fortune, founded during Elizabeth's reign by the swashbuckling Sir Rollo Stanton, was Sir Charles's to do with as he pleased, and he pleased to leave it in its entirety to his only child.

Naturally, the aunts were far too well bred to allow their disapproval of such an action to take the form of a vulgar display of chagrin, but it was the general consensus that there were other persons—and far more well equipped persons at that—to whom Sir Charles could have entrusted the care of his daughter and her fortune. Indeed without saying so in as many words, the ladies had been united in the view that had they known of their nephew's inconsiderate plans beforehand, they could have saved themselves an uncomfortable and, as it turned out, unnecessary journey into Wiltshire in the middle of what promised to be a particularly cold and damp October.

A rather breathless, wheezy voice interrupted Lucy's reverie. Scrubbing the damp tear stains from her cheeks she leapt to her feet, calling "Coming, Nanny."

Nanny Beckwith had been at Stanton Lacey for

fifty years. Now she was beginning to find the old house's many flights of stairs and long corridors tiring, and Lucy chided herself for forgetting that the aunts were likely to have sent someone after her. Nanny Beckwith's sister owned a small cottage in the village and she had confided to Lucy that she was looking forward to the day when she could share it with her.

"Like to like, Miss Lucy," was one of her favorite sayings. "We've grown old together, Emily and me, and we'll deal very well together when I'm gone from here."

Like to like . . . Lucy mused on the thought as she hurried downstairs. Was that why her father had decided to send her to Russia?

She could hear the aunts' voices still raised in outraged protest even before she opened the drawing room door. As she slipped into the room in her stark mourning—a small black wraith—she heard Aunt Maria saying peevishly,

"Well I don't know what Charles could have been thinking of. To send a single girl of good family all that way . . . and quite without any relative to support her . . ."

"Charles knew very well what he was doing," Aunt Jane commented acidly. "But whether he has done the right thing or not remains to be seen!"

She saw Lucy trying to slide unobtrusively into her chair and her frown deepened.

"There you are! Really Lucy, you are the most inconsiderate girl! We are all trying to discover how best we can comply with your father's wishes and you disappear! And your dress! It is quite dusty!"

Lucy repressed a small sigh. Truth to tell since her papa's death she had not paid much attention to her appearance. In his last moments before consciousness slid away from him, her father had made her promise not to shroud herself in black. Death brought him no pain save for leaving her, for he had every hope of being reunited with his dearest Nadia. Naturally, other people could not be expected to understand this last request, and so Nanny had run up a couple of drab, black gowns which Lucy wore without giving them any thought.

14

"I suppose we shall have to find some way of sending her to St. Petersburg," Aunt Maria commented disagreeably. "Trust Charles to go about things in such a ramshackled fashion. I told him years ago that he would be far better advised to send Lucy to a good seminary so that she could be brought up as befits a Stanton, but would he listen?"

Lucy had heard this grievance so many times before that she no longer paid any attention to it. Papa had mocked the education provided by the establishments recommended by Aunt Maria. Instead, he had set apart several hours a day ,which he devoted to teaching Lucy. Together they had perused the latest periodicals from London; together they had made the "Grand Tour" so fashionable a century ago, using great-grandfather Stanton's diaries for guides, Sir Charles endeavoring to make a game of the whole thing by insisting that they spoke only the language of the countries featured in the diaries. In this fashion Lucy learned French and Italian and thence progressed to Latin and Greek, thus enabling her to have the pleasure of reading the Classics in their original language.

"And your hair!" Aunt Jane commented critically. "Must it be so untidy?" Lucy started guiltily, delving in her reticule for pins to anchor her unruly locks but errant curls would keep escaping, framing her face in what, if she did but know it, was the most entrancing fashion.

"I've tried, Aunt Jane," she apologized.

"Umm, I suppose you think once you get to Russia you'll have a lady's maid to tend your every whim. Well let me warn you, Miss, you'll find life far different out there than it is here. I've heard that even the highest in the land are little better than savages." Jane murmured to her sisters. "They murder one another on the slightest whim, and I have it on the first authority that the Russian Ambassador has a slave who *actually* sleeps outside his bedroom door! In St. James's. Can you imagine it!"

Lucy pretended not to be listening. She and her father had often discussed Russia, and she realized now that he had probably been preparing her for what she might expect in her new country. Russians of consequence counted their wealth in the numbers of slaves they owned, a barbarous practice on the face of it, for surely no man but God had the right to own another man's soul. However, Lucy's papa had explained to her that a system existing for countless generations could not be overturned on the whim of a moment, no matter how appalling it might seem. Just as in England there were good and bad landlords, so in Russia there were good and bad, too. From his own experience he knew how devoted the serfs could be to their "owners" and how, in turn, the more far-sighted and humane members of the aristocracy took great pains to improve the lot of their serfs where they could. Alexander, himself, the Tsar of all Russia had made it known that he personally deplored serfdom; but so many of his people were little more than children, unable to fend for themselves without the protection of their masters. Enlightened people, so Sir Charles told his daughter, saw to it that their serfs were educated against the day when they might have the right to direct the course of their own lives.

Lucy and her father had also spent a considerable amount of time discussing Napoleon's campaigns in Egypt and Europe, and the War of Independence in America; thus Lucy had not placed any particular significance on what he had told her about Russia, save for having a very natural interest in the country that had been her mother's home.

"So what's to be done with the chit?" Aunt Rebecca asked with some exasperation.

"Well she can't travel to St. Petersburg alone." Aunt Jane replied practically. "Really one would think Charles would have had the sense to make proper arrangements, especially since it was his decision that Lucy go to Russia."

"Perhaps Count Vorontznov may be able to help?" Aunt Phoebe suggested timidly.

The other three stared at her. Phoebe seldom volunteered an opinion nor dared a suggestion. However, they all had to agree that she was showing unexpected good sense. If the Russian Ambassador could not help them, then no one could.

It was left to Aunt Jane to pronounce the final judgment. "Very well . . ." She drew on her black gloves as she spoke, glancing sharply at her sisters and niece. "I shall take Lucy back to London with me and approach the Russian Ambassador. It could well be that he might know of some person of quality who would undertake to escort Lucy to St. Petersburg."

The problem of their great-niece so happily disposed of and Lucy despatched to tell Nanny to pack a bag, the quartet fell once more to discussing the hitherto unsuspected laxness of their nephew.

"So very exciting don't you think?" Phoebe commented unwisely. "And so romantic!" Phoebe had what her sisters considered to be an unfortunate tendency toward "romanticism" which in her youth had led to a hopeless passion for a penniless guards officer she had met one summer in Bath. Naturally, the affair was doomed from the start. The gentleman in question was very much a "younger son" with his way to make in the world and certainly could never be considered as a match for a Stanton! Or so her papa had said, and Phoebe had dutifully agreed. Although there had been moments over the years when she had occasion to wonder if being the wife of a younger son—no matter how unworthy—might not have been preferable to being at the constant beck and call of her demanding sisters.

"Don't be so idiotish, Phoebe," Maria commented witheringly. "There is nothing in the least romantic about it. If Lucy has a scrap of sense, which I beg leave to doubt, she will tread very warily with these new-found relatives. It is a pity that he did not see fit to seek our advice. Only last season the Earl of Camberley was looking for a wife. He had only daughters from his first marriage and must needs get himself a son. It would have been an excellent match. But then it was ever Charles's way to act first and think last . . ."

Overhearing this part of the conversation on her return to the drawing room, Lucy felt an overwhelming surge of gratitude for papa's forethought. She had met the Earl of Camberley once when she and papa paid a visit to Aunt Maria, and she had disliked him excessively. Added to that he was three and fifty if he was a day!

Aunt Jane's London house was situated in Grosvenor Square. The hallway was fashionably stark with a black and white lozenge tiled floor and a narrow wrought iron staircase leading to the upper storeys. Lucy was greeted with a look of sympathy from Aunt Jane's butler, as he opened the door to them.

Pausing only to tell him to have tea sent up to her sitting room, Aunt Jane swept up the stairs, leaving Lucy to follow. Aunt Jane entertained a good deal, and the mantlepiece of Aunt Jane's boudoir was littered with unopened invitations and visiting cards. Bidding Lucy to sit down, she eyed her gown rather critically, remarking that she supposed she would have to do something about her clothes before she left for Russia.

"It is a thousand pities that your father should have died at this particular time," she remarked unfeelingly, "for you are far too old now to be confined to the school-room and yet you are not properly 'out.' Another six months and you could have made your curtsey. I had intended to speak to your father about it this Christmas. Of course there can be no question of a come-out now. Even if you were not going to Russia you would be in strict mourning for six months and then half mourning for another six, but then I expect you will find that your grandfather lives very quietly . . . . Lucy? Are you listening to me? Dear me, what will the Prince think of you? You may be sure he will not tolerate any silly daydreams. Now pull yourself together. Your uncle has left a message to say he will be dining out tonight. I suggest you retire early. I shall write a note to the Ambassador, and I can only hope he does not delay replying, for I have a good many pressing engagements.

Lucy just managed to bite back a bitter retort. If only papa were still alive, she thought despairingly a little later when she was curled up in bed. Her bedroom was cold, for Aunt Jane did not believe in unnecessary waste, and there was only the meanest of fires in the grate. It was a long time before sleep claimed her. Russia . . . . the word was on her tongue as she fell asleep, lonely tears still damp on her cheeks.

Lucy found herself left very much to her own devices while Aunt Jane fulfilled her various social obligations. Naturally, as she was in mourning Lucy could not accompany her, and although she did not normally find her own company a burden, she had to admit to finding time hanging heavily on her hands.

She spent one morning in Hookhams looking for books on Russia, and came away with half a dozen volumes purporting to be written by persons who knew the country and its people inside out. Even so, Lucy found it remarkably difficult to concentrate on the printed page when at last she retired to the library to read them.

On the third day after their arrival in London, Aunt Jane and Lucy were disturbed at breakfast by the entrance of the butler, bearing an impressively sealed letter on a silver tray, stamped with the crest of the Russian Ambassador.

Aunt Jane broke the seal and perused the letter before addressing herself to Lucy, who was trying to conceal her excited impatience by concentrating on her chocolate.

"The Ambassador suggests that we call upon him this afternoon. Apparently your grandfather has already been in touch with him and has sent someone to escort you to St. Petersburg."

She gave the information rather grudgingly, and Lucy hid a small smile. She knew quite well that her aunt would have been delighted had the Prince overlooked this small courtesy and left it to Lucy's paternal relatives to arrange her journey. It seemed her fears that her grandfather might have had second thoughts about welcoming her into his family were completely unfounded. All at once Lucy began to feel a good deal happier. She couldn't wait for the afternoon to come. There were so many things she wanted to know; so many questions she had to ask.

"Lucy, stop daydreaming, and tell Alice to press your other black gown. The Princess Lieven was telling me last night that you will need thick furs and stout boots for the journey. I have a fitting with Celeste tomorrow, we will have to see what she can do for you. I suppose it's too much to expect your grandfather to remember that you will need suitable clothes," she remarked disagreeably.

Lucy was glad to escape from the table. Upstairs in her room she studied her reflection rather ruefully. Even the plain black gown could not dim the radiance of her smile or the pearly whiteness of her skin, but she noticed none of these things. Instead she concentrated on taming her unruly ringlets, and offering up a small prayer that life in St. Petersburg would not be as difficult as life in London. She knew Aunt Jane meant well, and that it was second nature for her to be forever complaining; but apart from the normal polite condolences, none of the aunts seemed to realize how much she missed her father, or how alone and strange she felt away from the protective familiarity of Stanton Lacey.

Two

Shortly after lunch it started to rain, a fine unceasing drizzle which turned the whole landscape gray. It was unseasonably cold for October and Lucy was glad of the hot brick at her feet as she sat next to Aunt Jane in the carriage. Already, most of the trees in the squares had lost their leaves, and there was an air of damp depression everywhere, so in accord with her own mood since her father's death, that she longed to get away from London.

The Ambassador's residence was a white stuccoed building looking out over the park. Two liveried footmen bowed them into a square hall hung with a priceless crystal chandelier. One of the Ambassador's aides escorted them to a large anteroom furnished in gold satin. "The Count will be with you shortly," he promised them as he withdrew. A large fire was burning in the grate and although Aunt Jane sniffed disparagingly over the wastefulness of heating such a huge room for two people, Lucy noticed that she was soon drawing her chair nearer to its cheering blaze.

They weren't kept waiting very long, although to Lucy, already in a state of extreme nervousness, it seemed a veritable lifetime. Certainly it was long enough for Aunt Jane to comment denigratingly on the quality of the decor and to examine rather triumphantly the small icon hanging on the wall. "I hear their religious practices are little short of barbaric . . ." she was commenting to Lucy when the door was opened by a footman and the Ambassador stepped in.

He was not at all what Lucy had expected. He looked no different from any other gentleman of her father's generation, although to be sure his clothes were a good deal finer, but there was none of the lavish love of display that Aunt Jane's acerbic comments had led her to expect. He was rather rotund and slightly balding, and Lucy thought she detected an unexpected twinkle in his eye when he took her hand.

"So you are Nadia Ivanovna's daughter. You are very like her. Ivan Ivanovich, Prince Kuragin, your grandfather, has instructed me to waste no time in sending you to St. Petersburg. Soon it will be winter there." He sighed reminiscently, "Much as I love London, I confess to a longing to be back in St. Petersburg. Ivan Ivanovich informs me that the Grand Duchess Sophy Petronovna, who is what you would call his sister-in-law, is to sponsor you in society. You will like her."

Aunt Jane clicked her tongue. "My dear count, such outlandish names as you have! It was quite a surprise to us to discover that Lucy had relatives living in Russia. Her father never spoke one word about them to us I can assure you; otherwise my sisters and I would have done all we could to persuade him to heal the breach. Tell me, this escort the Prince has sent for Lucy, I take it you can vouch. . . ." She let the sentence hang delicately for a few moments, while the Ambassador's eyebrows shot up.

"My dear Madam, please be assured that the gentleman concerned has my personal recommendation, little though he needs it. Prince Kuragin has sent his grandson, Prince Nikolai Andreyevich Kuragin to escort Miss Stanton to Russia. The Prince is a colonel in the Tsar's own personal regiment, the Preobrajensky Guards; in fact I don't think I'm betraying a confidence when I tell you that the Prince is numbered among the Tsar's intimates."

Lucy gave a rather wan smile. Her confidence was being more and more depleted with every passing second. Princess, Grand Duchesses—her head was swimming with titles.

22

As though he knew what she was thinking, the Ambassador smiled reassuringly and glanced at his watch. "I am expecting the Prince any moment. I believe he already has all the arrangements for your journey in hand; but I am sure he will wish to discuss these with you himself. It is unfortunate that you are obliged to travel now, when winter is setting in; but you need have no fear with Nikolai Andreyevich as your escort."

"I trust this gentleman will not be long delayed," Aunt Jane was saying with a frown. "I promised to call on Lady Sefton this afternoon and it is gone three already . . ."

"If you wish to continue to Lady Sefton's, I can undertake to send Miss Stanton back to Grosvenor Street in one of my carriages when she has spoken with her cousin."

Aunt Jane frowned again and glanced rather sharply at Lucy's averted profile. Lucy already knew what she was thinking. It was unheard of for a young lady to be alone with a gentleman to whom she had only just been introduced; but since, in this case, the gentleman concerned was also her cousin, the normal rules of polite society could hardly be held to apply. However, Aunt Jane decided to remain.

"I trust the Prince has brought some female with him who can chaperone you while you are in his care, for I cannot spare anyone from my own household to go with you, even should they be willing, which I am sure they would not!" she finished dampeningly.

Lucy knew she was blushing with embarrassment, but the Ambassador continued to smile kindly at her. "I'm sure, Madam, you need have no fears for Miss Stanton's reputation while she is in her cousin's care. In Russia it is quite acceptable for a young lady to travel with a male relative unchaperoned; indeed it is sometimes necessary, when weather conditions make it impossible to travel with vast numbers of servants. No, don't look alarmed, Miss Stanton," he added when he saw Lucy's widening eyes and slight frown. "It's just that I happen to know that the Prince is anxious to lose no time

23

in returning to St. Petersburg. He will of necessity wish to travel light. It will be your first taste of travelling over snow-bound territory in a sleigh, but I am sure you will enjoy it."

A servant came in and murmured something to the Ambassador who straightened up and smiled. "The Prince has arrived. The footman will show him in"

His smile to Lucy was both understanding and re-assuring, as though he knew of her fears, and she took courage from it, composing herself to meet this cousin she had not even known existed. Obviously he must be her grandfather's heir. How would he feel about her? Would he resent her intrusion into the family circle?

The door opened and the man who strode in made Lucy catch a small gasp of dismay. He looked so proud and cold, ignoring both Lucy and her aunt, and instead smiling briefly at the Ambassador. He was much taller than the Count, somewhere in his early thirties, Lucy guessed, although his arrogant demeanor made him seem older. His hair was as dark as her own, and fashionably disordered. However, it was his eyes that caught and held Lucy's dismayed attention. Dark green, they were frozen and empty of expression, reminding her of the jade carvings a previous Stanton had brought back from the East.

The Ambassador performed the introductions, and Lucy's small curtsey was acknowledged with the briefest inclination of the dark head in a gesture of arrogant disdain.

While Aunt Jane complained endlessly about her nephew's inexplicable desire for Lucy to go to Russia, Lucy looked down at the floor; but it was impossible not to be aware of the merciless scrutiny to which she was being subjected, and when at last the cold gaze was with-drawn she felt as though she had not a single thought left unviolated by that arctic stare. It was a chastening experi-ence, and she felt the first beginnings of a deep anger start to stir within her. He had no right, no right at all, to look at her so disparagingly. Her own fiery pride responded to his icy contempt like fire to dry tinder. Her small hands curled into minute fists and she glared

24

mutinously at the hard, thin line of his mouth. His features were partially masked by the shadows, but she caught the sardonic lift of his eyebrows as he registered her reaction, and it added fresh fuel to her anger.

"Well, Lucy, I shall leave you to become acquainted with your cousin," Aunt Jane said briskly as she made to leave them. "It is most fortunate that your grandfather thought to make these arrangements, for I am sure I don't know quite how we would have gone on otherwise." She nodded dismissively in the direction of the Prince and extended her hand to the Ambassador. They withdrew together and when they had gone, a peculiar silence seemed to fall on the room. Lucy could not remember ever having felt so acutely uncomfortable in all her life!"

"Please be seated cousin," her new relative drawled. It was a command rather than a request, and, angry though she was, Lucy found herself complying with it. He himself took up a stance before the fire, an impressive figure in pale fawn pantaloons and shiny Hessian boots. He was wearing a dark blue jacket of some fine wool material and Lucy stared wonderingly at his broad shoulders. Her look was returned with bored indifference.

Lucy did not have as much experience of the opposite sex as other girls of her age and birth; but she knew well enough when she was being condescended to, and her chin lifted. That her cousin was an extremely handsome man she did not deny, but that did not prevent him from being cold and haughty. She searched his features for a spark of warmth and finding none, summoned a manner every bit as disdainfully chilly as her companion's.

"I trust you left my grandfather in good health, Prince?" she asked formally, staring at a spot somewhere to the left of her cousin's forbidding shoulders.

"I did," he agreed curtly, "although I cannot conceive what possible interest our grandfather's health is to you."

While Lucy was absorbing this snub, he continued coldly, "And you will not call me 'Prince.' We are cousins and you will refer to me as 'Nikolai' or 'Nikolai Andreyevich,' should you be feeling particularly affectionate!"

25

"Nikolai will suffice, cousin," Lucy responded trying to mask her anger, and making a mental vow never to refer to her cousin as "Nikolai Andreyevich, which was how the Ambassador had addressed him and was, as Lucy knew from her father's patient teaching a familiar form of address meaning "Nikolai son of Andrei."

"As you wish." He shrugged indifferently as though it were of scant importance.

Before Lucy could comment on his earlier snub, he continued decisively: "And please spare me any further professions of interest in our mutual grandparents." He smiled scathingly, his eyes hard. "I am not an old man to be easily gulled by a pretty face."

"No, you are not." Lucy agreed vehemently. "You are cold and hard . . . and . . ." To her horror she felt tears welling in her eyes, and as she turned away she heard Nikolai's acid comment:

"Just as I suspected. Pert, ill-mannered and I expect completely uneducated. What are you hoping for from Russia, cousin? A rich husband?"

Before Lucy could deny this accusation, he switched suddenly to French, throwing half a dozen questions at her in quick succession. She answered automatically and had the satisfaction of seeing the black brows snap together over the proud nose, as though their owner had just received a disagreeable shock. Lucy knew her French was good. Papa had seen to that. He had also told her that it was the principal language of the Russian aristocracy. Now she knew why. The thought of her father brought fresh tears to her eyes. In an effort to distract Nikolai's all too sharp eyes from this sign of weakness, Lucy asked challengingly:

"Is my grandfather as reluctant to welcome me into his family as you? If so you may return alone!"

For a moment she thought she saw grudging respect in Nikolai's eyes, and then it was gone.

"Grandpère is besotted at the thought of having you under his roof," came the terse reply. "But he is not as astute as he once was, and I will not have him taken in by a pert miss hoping to catch herself a rich husband."

Lucy's eyes flashed. His arrogance took her breath away. For two pins she would tell him just how little need she had of a wealthy husband, but instead she counted to ten and concentrated on a particularly excellent water coloring adorning the opposite wall.

"The Fontanka Canal," her tormentor said unexpectedly, coming to stand behind her. "In winter the Neva and the canal freeze and St. Petersburg society flocks to the ice to skate and flirt and eat blinis hot from the vendors' stand."

It was an unexpectedly lifelike glimpse of another world and Lucy longed to ask more, but pride held her aloof.

"It sounds quite charming," she said instead, in a very fair imitation of her aunt's grand manner, and had the satisfaction of seeing his eyes narrow consideringly as they rested on her face. She did not tell him that she herself had learned to skate one hard winter on the lake at Stanton Lacey or how surprised the village children had been at her unexpected skill.

"There are several matters we must discuss before we leave London," Nikolai continued, as though she had not spoken. His voice was deep and pleasant, yet for some reason it contrived to jar on Lucy's over-strung nerves. With growing dismay she acknowledged that she was already well on the way to disliking this new cousin, and they had not yet spent half an hour in each other's company. She looked up, intending to make some idle comment, but the words were forgotten as Nikolai moved fractionally and the light from the windows fell sharply on his face highlighting the long white scar that ran from temple to jaw.

"Unpleasant, isn't it?" Tanned fingers traced the thin line. "A legacy from a duel, fought before the Tsar forbade them. We are a people whose blood runs hot, Lucy Stanton, and you would do well to remember that; you whose blood has been thinned by the cautious Englishness of your father. As for the scar . . . you will grow accustomed to it, as I have, and I beg only that you do not allow our grandfather to see your revulsion. He does not like to

27

be reminded of how I acquired it. Now, let us return to the arrangements for our journey."

The scar was dismissed as lightly as though it were no more than some slight cut, but Lucy sensed that behind the cold demeanor her cousin was deeply sensitive about the thin, pale line. She stole a glance at the aloof profile. A duel he had said. Over what? A woman? Surely not. A matter of honor more likely. He was a man who would hold his honor very dear indeed.

"If you would kindly give me your attention . . ." The sarcastic voice bit into the silence. "I have chartered a vessel to convey us to Tilsit. From there we shall travel by sleigh to St. Petersburg. If we are lucky the entire journey should be completed within the month. During that time you will obey me implicitly in all things, for the land we shall be traversing is a hostile one, where the price of your defiance could well be your life . . ."

Words of protest died on Lucy's lips when she saw that he was serious and despite the warmth of the room she shivered as though already feeling the cold wind of the steppes.

"We leave London in a sennight's time. I have prepared a list of all that you will require." The black gown came under the formidable stare, and was quite obviously found lacking. "Grandpère will not like to see you so attired," Nikolai told her disparagingly. "You would do well to purchase something more flattering before you leave London."

Anger overcome her good resolutions.

"I am sorry if my grandfather finds the fact that I am in mourning for my father distasteful, but I shall continue to wear it until the period of my mourning is over." Even as she spoke Lucy knew that her father would have been in complete agreement with Nikolai, but anger rose within her on a swift tide, drowning out reason. "Or perhaps I mistake the matter, and you are trying to warn me not to expect to find the latest fashions in St. Petersburg . . ."

"Far from it. We take our fashions direct from Paris, cousin Lucy. You will find every other lady arrayed in

28

the thinnest of muslins *a la directoire,* despite the fact that Bonaparte is on the point of invading us. Nothing must be allowed to stand in a lady's way of ensnaring her latest victim, even if she has to suffer a putrid sore throat from dampened skirts to achieve it." Under the contempt lay a savage anger, barely held in check and Lucy wondered at its cause, even while her own proud spirit rose to counter the accusation he had just flung at her sex.

"You seem to have a very low opinion of my sex," she said lightly, "and I can only suppose the blame for that lies at your own feet. If men will prefer beauty to brains, they are justly served by the results of that preference."

"What are you advocating? A man looks for pleasure in a woman, not instruction," he informed her brutally. "And if you intend to get yourself a husband you had best remember as much."

Several moments later when the Ambassador tapped discreetly on the door and opened it, he found them standing with the entire width of the fine Aubusson carpet between them, the air thick with the kind of silence which follows or precedes a less than cordial exchange.

When Lucy had been sent safely on her way, the Ambassador entered his study where Nikolai was waiting for him.

The younger man was standing with his back to him, staring out into the rain be-spattered street.

"A charming child, and very like her mother . . . spirited too, although naturally the death of her father had left her subdued. Whoever takes charge of her will doubtless find himself with his hands full."

"Meaning me I assume?" Nikolai commented in neutral accents. "For that is what it will come down to. Sophy is about as capable of keeping her under control as a babe in arms."

"She is a young lady, Nikolai, not a horse," the Ambassador commented mildly. He was trying very hard to hide his amusement. He had known the Kuragin family for many years, and remembering Nadia at Lucy's age

29

had been immediately struck by the likeness between them. "She is the image of her mother," he said, more to himself than to his companion, fortunately, though, there was no likelihood of history repeating itself. The old Prince had learned his lesson; there would be no arranged marriage for Lucy.

"Do you have the reports for the Tsar?" Nikolai asked, ignoring the Ambassador's reference to Lucy. Sensing that particular subject was now closed, and knowing his companion, the Ambassador regretfully dismissed Lucy from his mind and turned it instead to more weighty matters. "Yes. They are here, ready for you. Our spies in France report that they are convinced Bonaparte intends to try and invade Russia. After our past defeats he is convinced that . . . ." he broke off, remembering that the young man at his side had taken part in those battles and had seen his friends die before his eyes. "How are they taking it in St. Petersburg?" he asked, and then changing the subject, "Or do they still believe that Bonaparte will never dare risk crossing the Nieven?"

"They are like children, living from day to day, concerned only with the transient glisten of the moment— you know that. For the present the Tsar is content that it should be so. There are too many people in positions of authority who would gladly sue the French for peace. He does not want to provoke any more problems than he already has."

The light from the chandelier emphasized his scar, tautening the skin of his face, and the Ambassador sighed. A difficult, proud man, and a lonely one he suspected. For all his good looks he had a coldness that froze even the most forward flirt, and they said in St. Petersburg that he was as cold as a Russian winter, impervious to the failings that beset other men. The Ambassador did not envy Lucy Stanton, his enforced companionship. The girl would need every ounce of her undeniable spirit.

"I know you do not want to tarry any longer than necessary, Nikolai. My secretary will give you the reports. It only remains for me to wish you a good journey. Please convey my respects to your grandfather. I am sure Miss Stanton will bring much pleasure to his life."

"And possibly much pain," the Prince commented cryptically fingering his scar. "How could it be otherwise? She is a female and I doubt not extremely foolish."

Four days before the time appointed for their departure. Lucy received a curt note from her cousin reminding her that their ship would be sailing at high tide and that if she proposed to indulge in the female delight of arriving late, he would have to sail without her.

The messenger had also brought a cumbersome package which, when unwrapped and denuded of its layers of tissue paper, turned out to be a traveling cloak in some fine woollen fabric which was unfamiliar to Lucy. It was the inside of the cloak, though, that caused her to gasp in wonder, for it was lined with thick, glossy furs. Aunt Jane, who was sitting at her desk, writing to appraise her sisters of Lucy's imminent departure turned, her eyes widening in envy as she saw what her great-niece was holding in trembling hands.

"Sables! And extremely fine ones by the look of them. It must have cost a fortune!"

"There is a note with it," Lucy told her shakily. "The Prince . . . my cousin . . . says I will need it for the journey, and that it is my grandfather's gift to me!"

"Quite unsuitable for a girl of your years," Aunt Jane pronounced dampeningly. "And far too ostentatious. . . ."

But Lucy wasn't listening. Clasping the cloak in her arms, her cheek resting on the glossy furs, she was lost in her own private daydreams. A smile trembled on her lips, and her tender heart was touched to think of her grandfather buying this gift for her, perhaps as nervous about their first meeting as she was herself.

In no time at all the morning of her departure arrived, dawning cold and clear. Shivering over her ablutions Lucy made haste to dress, trying to suppress the quivers of mingled excitement and fear tingling through her.

31

Her trunk was already packed. She had followed Nikolai's instructions to the letter about the sort of garments she would require, although she had occasionally wondered how he came to have such an intimate knowledge of female apparel. On one point, however, she had remained obdurate. She had stuck to her mourning colors, only weakening over a charming carriage dress of palest lilac with a matching, fur trimmed bonnet and then only because Aunt Jane had insisted that she needed at least one decent dress if her grandfather wasn't to think her a charity case.

Now the lilac gown was packed away in her trunk, and Aunt Jane was congratulating herself that out of the large sum Sir Charles had set aside for equipping his daughter for her journey, there was ample left over to complete the refurbishment of her own wardrobe. As she had constantly repeated to Lucy, there was little point in purchasing expensive blacks, with nearly four months of her mourning already past.

She had further eased her conscience by saying that once she arrived in St. Petersburg, Lucy would undoubtedly find that her grandfather expected her to go into half mourning, for he would be bound to want to introduce her to his friends and that he could not do if she persisted in sticking rigidly to the conventions.

Lucy had suppressed a rather wry smile. It was the first time she had ever heard one of the aunts decry convention. As to her lack of expensive gowns—if the truth were told Lucy much preferred the few simple dresses she already owned to the expensive creations produced by Celeste. The enormity of the step she was taking was beginning to take its toll on her, and she was constantly beset by an absurd desire to fling herself into her uncle's arms and plead to be allowed to stay with them.

After only the merest morsel of breakfast she followed Aunt Jane out to the waiting carriage, trying not to think that this might be the last time she traversed the familiar streets.

The brigantine Nikolai had commissioned for their journey lay at her moorings, a round, squat vessel with a hull designed to cope with northern winters and icy seas. She looked singularly unglamorous, and Lucy was not reassured when a bearded stranger hefted her trunk onto his shoulders and bore it away up a narrow gangplank.

"Your cousin is late," Aunt Jane reproved as though Lucy were personally responsible for Nikolai's tardiness, but the words had barely left her lips when a curricle drove up alongside their carriage and Nikolai jumped out.

At first Lucy hardly recognized him. Gone was the elegant gentleman of fashion she had met in the Ambassador's drawing room, and in his place stood an imposing stranger dressed in riding breeches and thigh-length boots, a sable-lined cloak draped carelessly over one shoulder, the thick, black hair blowing freely in the wind.

He greeted Lucy coolly, throwing an instruction to the man following him as he reached for Lucy's arm. Aunt Jane was dismissed with a curt nod, and left standing on the flagway.

"This is my servant, Feodor," Nikolai announced as he hurried Lucy toward the ship. "He will take care of your needs as well as mine while we are traveling; and before you go all Missish on me, rest assured that it is quite the common thing at home."

At home! Lucy savored the words, trying to draw comfort from them, as the ship slipped its moorings and the Thames bore them toward the open sea.

Her cabin was tiny, but she did have a porthole. She could hear Feodor moving about in the adjoining cabin, which was Nikolai's and so was reassured that she had not been totally deserted. She wished she and Nikolai might have been better friends, but it was obviously not to be.

Fortunately, Lucy proved to be a good sailor, although they were lucky with the weather. She felt Nikolai would have had scant patience or sympathy with a seasick female. The only time they spent more than a few minutes at a stretch in one another's company was in the evening when they dined with the captain. If the word "dined" could be used in the context of the tough salt beef and half raw potatoes that seemed to comprise the ship's cook's sole culinary offering.

Feodor, Nikolai's servant, was the only person who seemed to have the time to answer her rather hesitant questions; and although Lucy felt rather guilty about encouraging the man to gossip about his master, she suspected that Feodor enjoyed the opportunity of boasting about Nikolai's achievements as much as she enjoyed hearing about life in Russia.

Beneath the cold, proud face he showed to the world, Lucy sensed a bitterness in her cousin that commanded her pity even while she wondered at its cause. He made it obvious that he held her sex in the greatest contempt and never seemed to miss an opportunity to make some sardonic retort to anything she might have to say, but she did not know why. One thing she did know though was that Nikolai would have scant use for her pity and no doubt his cool, dry voice would rebuff her if she was ever foolish enough to voice it.

Feodor gave her the first clue to the reason for the air of cold hauteur that clung to her cousin. He was sitting outside the cabin door, polishing his master's boots when Lucy chanced to walk past, pausing to admire his diligence.

They were two days out of Tilsit where they were to disembark and proceed overland to St. Petersburg by sleigh pulled by the teams of horses Nikolai kept at every halt along the way.

Feodor beamed with pleasure when Lucy marvelled at the shine he had achieved. At first she had been a little nervous of him with his thick, bushy beard and intense devotion to Nikolai, but fear had soon given way to affection. Now he told her with justifiable pride that there wasn't a finer pair of boots in all the Regiment. "Nor a finer master," he added loyally, "for all that some are pleased to say about him. The old Prince thinks the world of him, and well he might. There isn't a serf on his estates that wouldn't lay down his life for him."

Lucy wondered what it was that "some were pleased to say about him," but decided against questioning Feodor more deeply lest he unwittingly betray her interest to Nikolai in an unguarded moment. "It is strange that he is not married . . ." she commented, more to herself than to Feodor, "for surely my grandfather will want to see the name continue?"

As her father's only child no one knew the importance of *that* more than she, but Feodor ceased his task and eyed her, his head on one side. "There was to be a marriage once, but it all came to nothing. Plenty of time for him to marry yet, but not to the likes of her," he added obliquely. "She did not care for him as a wife should; she cared only for money and social position. He is better off without her. But marry he will, make no mistake about that; he won't want to disappoint the old Prince." He talked about the family with all the familiarity of a very old retainer and Lucy was to learn that the gulf between servant and master in Russia was not as well defined as it was in England. In Russia a servant could and often did take part in his better's conversation, rather like a privileged nanny with her adult nurslings.

With nothing to do but sit and stare at the North Sea—for her books were safely stored in her trunk to prevent any risk of mildewing—it was only natural that Lucy's thoughts should linger on the marriage that might have been. Had her cousin been bitterly hurt when his lady rejected him? She repressed a small smile. It was difficult to imagine such a circumstance. Nikolai was impervious to attack through his emotions, any wife of his would need to be a meek, self-effacing creature prepared to spend her life on her husband's country estates, favored every now and again by the occasional visit to replenish the nurseries. Lucy chided herself for her less than generous train of thought; but it was true—she decided defiantly, Nikolai was arrogant and unfeeling and deserved to go through life without giving or receiving love.

Although Lucy was not well versed in the arts of flirtation, she knew instinctively that when she loved, it would be as her mother had done: passionately and wholeheartedly, giving her all; and that once given her love could never be reclaimed.

From the odd hints Feodor dropped, she gained the

impression that while her cousin had no room in his life for love, he was not a total stranger to some of the pleasures of the flesh, for Feodor was constantly sprinkling his conversation with references to visits to the gypsy dancers to listen to wild music and watch the dark-eyed women dancing, or to the theatre where troups of serfs were trained to perform the latest plays for their masters.

Lucy was not so innocent that she could not guess at the sort of liaisons that sprang up between the young men who watched these performances and the young women who gave them. Papa had never censored her reading, explaining to her that understanding and compassion for her fellow-men came only from knowledge of the forces that sometimes drove them.

Thus, she now reasoned that it was no business of hers if her cousin chose to keep a mistress, nor indeed if he chose to keep half a dozen; but she was curious to know if anything other than anger could ever darken those piercing green eyes or if that hard mouth could ever soften from its sardonically bitter smile. On balance Lucy decided that it was more unlikely than likely, and to compensate for what she knew to be ill-bred curiosity, she diverted Feodor's reminiscences away from tales of the gypsies and instead bade him tell her about the Winter Palace and the Tsar.

Feodor was nothing loath. Like the Ambassador, he informed her that her cousin was a close confidant of the Tsar, and that even when Nikolai was not on duty he tended to spend a good deal of his time in attendance upon Alexander.

"Apart from when he goes to Moscow in the summer, or when the Regiment is on manoeuvres at Gatchina,"

"Gatchina?"

"The barracks designed by the present Tsar's father," Feodor explained to Lucy. "The Regiment to which Nikolai Andreyevich belongs is the Tsar's own, and very fine too, he looks in his uniform, with the Order of St. Andrew across his chest. You will like St. Petersburg, Lucy Ivanovna!" This was how Feodor had taken to addressing Lucy, and secretly she found it rather touching. The manservant's brown eyes twinkled. "There will be many young men anxious to dance with you when you are presented at the Winter Palace. What a pity the Tsar already has a wife . . . ."

"You are filling my cousin's head with nonsense, Feodor."

Nikolai had come up behind them so quietly that neither of them had heard him arrive. Lucy started guiltily hoping he had not guessed that he had been the subject of their conversation.

"Feodor is merely telling me about St. Petersburg," she explained hurriedly, allowing her tone to hint that if he had bestirred himself in that direction instead of spending all his time with the captain, there would have been no need for Feodor to tell her anything.

"I don't doubt it. But if his information contained the advice that the Tsar might be persuaded to glance in your direction, I should warn you not to take it," he said depressingly. "Not only does the Tsar have a wife, he also has an extremely beautiful Polish mistress."

There was nothing in his voice to betray whether he approved or disapproved of this state of affairs, but Lucy knew immediately where her sympathies lay.

"How very fortunate he is; but then, of course, if gentlemen may do as they please in these matters, then how much more so must Emperors."

"You would be well advised not to voice such sentiments abroad in St. Petersburg," Nikolai cautioned her coldly. "The Tsar is an enlightened ruler by Russian standards, but he will brook no criticism of his morals by a chit still wet behind the ears. It seems to me," he added cuttingly, "that when your father educated you he omitted to include a lesson on the value of good manners."

He turned on his heel, but Lucy, furious at his criticism of her beloved Papa, retorted hotly,

"Oh but you mistake the matter cousin. Naturally I know the value of good manners, but I have decided to take a leaf out of your book and not waste them on a mere relative, for it seems we are destined to see only the worst of one another!"

"I believe I already know the worst of you!" came Nikolai's icy rejoinder. "Namely, that you are as foolishly empty-headed as one might expect from a female of your years and lack of experience. Unfortunately, it seems you choose to exacerbate these faults by adopting a manner which cannot fail to cause one to remark that your father must have quitted this life with very little regret. And now," he added grimly, "perhaps you will listen to what I came down here to tell you in the first place. The captain reports that our voyage should be at an end tomorrow. Be so good as to be ready to leave the ship by then."

Lucy watched him go through a haze of tears. How many times had papa warned her to keep a guard on her too quick tongue! How stupid she had been to throw herself open to being labelled malapert, or even worse, but Nikolai's attitude towards her seemed to bring out a side of her nature she had never known she possessed. Self-willed, the aunts had often called her, and there was a grain of truth in the accusation, but never before had she fallen into the error of betraying herself into behavior such as to call down upon her head the accusations her cousin had so lately levelled at her.

It seemed they could not meet without quarrelling, she reflected soberly, and they could not quarrel without Nikolai making some defamatory remark about her sex as a whole and herself in particular! All of which inclined her to the view that for the sake of family harmony it would be as well if the two of them were not constrained to share the same roof for any length of time!

Three

It was much colder in Tilsit than it had been in London. Nikolai glanced at the leaden sky and remarked ominously that it was a pity they had not arrived sooner as it seemed that winter had beaten them to it.

It was strange to feel dry land beneath her feet again after so many days at sea, and Lucy huddled gratefully in her fur-lined coat as she waited for Feodor to find a sleigh to take them to the inn where they were to spend the night preparatory to commencing their journey to St. Petersburg.

"Don't expect the same standards as you would from the 'George' on Dover road," Nikolai warned her. "Conditions are very rough and ready."

He had not been exaggerating as Lucy discovered when the sleigh deposited them outside the shabby wooden building. Inside, the atmosphere was thick with smoke from the pot-bellied stoves around which groups of travellers were clustered. In fact, it was so bad for the first few minutes Lucy's eyes smarted to such an extent that it was impossible for her to see properly.

Even so, it was bliss to bathe again if only in the stout wooden tub drawn up before her bedroom fire. A giggling maid was on hand to ladle hot water over her, and Lucy had to repress a small smile at the thought of the aunts' reactions to such hopelessly medieval customs.

Downstairs Feodor had prepared a meal for them,

and while they ate Lucy stole a few discreet glances at their fellow travellers.

A troupe of gypsies were laughing and talking in one corner. Four Hussars stood in front of the fire, discussing something in low voices. As Lucy watched, one of the Hussars glanced up and saw the gypsies. He made some comment to his companions and then sauntered across to join them.

One of the gypsies picked up a balalaika and resting his foot on a small stool started to sing softly: his voice raw and slightly husky, vibrating with a harsh undercurrent of passion as he glanced at the woman at his feet.

Lucy pushed away the remains of her meal to listen, shivering a little under the assault of the wild, demanding music filling the room.

As the throbbing tempo of the music increased the woman uncurled herself, as sinuously graceful as a cat, arching her body in time to the gypsy tune. As she danced, her full red skirts swirled around her like the crimson petals of a rose. Faster and faster she whirled, until Lucy felt dizzy.

One by one the other gypsies joined the solitary dancer. Lucy felt her own heartbeats increase in time to the music and her blood seemed to be tingling through her body, urging her toward the verge of some, as yet unknown emotion.

In the candlelight she wasn't aware of Nikolai's eyes narrowing slightly as he watched her absorbed, rapt profile.

"I think it's time you went to bed," he told her abruptly. "We shall need an early start in the morning."

Lucy started to protest, but he had destroyed her enjoyment. Her earlier euphoria was gone, leaving her curiously flat and drained. She bade him goodnight, rather stiffly, and went upstairs to her room without a backward look. The atmosphere in the cramped bedroom was stifling, and she longed to be able to open a window. Downstairs the gypsies still danced and sang. Perhaps it was that that caused her to sleep so badly and wake up with heavy eyes and an aching head.

She arrived downstairs to find Nikolai, his breakfast already over. He was standing in the now empty room, staring frowningly out through the window, his cloak flung carelessly over the back of a chair. He greeted her brusquely and seemed impatient to be gone.

Lucy was just finishing the cup of coffee Feodor had brought her when there was a small commotion by the door. A woman swept in—there could be no other way to describe her entrance—wrapped from head to foot in sables, the hood of her cloak flung back to reveal blonde ringlets and a classically beautiful profile.

"Nikolai!"

At close range, she was older than Lucy had first supposed. There were fine lines around her rather shallow blue eyes, and when she wasn't smiling her mouth turned downward in petulant dissatisfaction. She ignored Lucy, chattering excitedly to Nikolai in French, her small, white, hand resting on his arm. From the conversation Lucy learned that she had just arrived in Tilsit and that she was travelling to England to visit friends.

"Elizabeth, let me introduce you to my cousin," Nikolai said when there was a break in the conversation.

She eyed Lucy coldly, and gave her a thin, dismissive smile, turning back to Nikolai.

"So that is the result of poor Nadia's mesalliance. She has her looks." She shrugged contemptuously. "Let us hope she does not share her taste for parvenus."

Lucy checked a protest, unable to believe she was hearing correctly. "No doubt the father hoped to use her to ingratiate himself with your grandfather. Perhaps he even hoped that the Prince would settle enough on her to enable her to make a good marriage." Her tone suggested that such an outcome was more than unlikely. Lucy's body stiffened in outrage.

"My father was *not* a parvenu," she announced in faultlessly clear French. "Neither is there any need for me to go begging to my grandfather or anyone else."

Elizabeth's thin eyebrows rose distastefully, her mouth a small moue of knowing contempt.

"My dear Nikolai, where was the child brought up?

Someone really must look to her manners. If it is true that she does have a respectable position, you must take care to guard her from fortune hunters. Those who hold the name of Kuragin in respect would be sorry to see two such unsuitable marriages in as many generations."

"How dare you speak so about my father," Lucy burst out passionately. "He was good . . . kind . . ."

"That will do," Nikolai interrupted in an expressionless voice. "You will apologize and at once!"

"Only if your—friend—apologizes first, for her remarks about my father," Lucy retorted stubbornly.

Truth to tell she was already regretting her unseemly outburst, but she could not stand meekly aside and hear her father spoken of so. She allowed her lip to curl slightly in an excellent imitation of Aunt Jane's famous style and drawled in a voice quite as langorous as Elizabeth's. "If seems to me, *cousin,* that, contrary to what you would have me believe, bad manners are not the sole perquisite of the British!"

Elizabeth gave a tinkling laugh, glancing uneasily from Lucy's small, set face to Nikolai's hard, cold one.

Lucy knew quite well that Nikolai was aware of the meaning behind her comment, but he chose to ignore it, instead informing her in clipped accents which didn't quite manage to hide his anger, that he was still waiting to hear Lucy's apology.

She remained steadfast, even under the ice-cold look he was giving her.

In the end it was Elizabeth who broke the uncomfortable silence. "Oh please, Nikolai, let's forget it." She gave Lucy a malevolent look. "Poor Sophy, it seems she is going to have her hands full."

She raised herself on tiptoe and kissed Nikolai on both cheeks. "Miss Stanton is not as much like her Mama as I had supposed. Dearest Nadia had the sweetest nature imaginable!"

With this parting shot she mounted the stairs, half a dozen serfs toiling behind her with a huge trunk.

When she had gone the silence became oppressive.

42

Lucy glowered determinedly into her coffee cup, her hands curled into minute, protesting fists.

"The next time you decide to treat me to a display of your appalling manners, you may be sure that I shall take the necessary action to curtail it—and speedily," Nikolai said curtly at last.

Her manners?" What about Elizabeth's? Lucy's blood boiled in furious resentment. Her soft mouth tightened as she lifted her eyes and looked furiously at him. "By doing what?" she demanded loftily.

His reply, when it came, caught her completely off guard and brought an indignant flush to her cheeks. "By putting you over my knee and administering a punishment sharp enough to prevent you from sitting down in comfort for a sennight!"

"You wouldn't dare!"

But the disturbing glint in his eyes warned that not only would he dare, but that he would probably derive the utmost enjoyment from doing so as well.

"And what about your friend, Elizabeth? Is she to be punished in the same way?"

He did not pretend to misunderstand. "Elizabeth's behavior is no concern of mine. She is not a member of my family, and now, if you have quite finished making a spectacle of yourself, Feodor is here with the sleighs."

"Sleighs?" Lucy was puzzled.

"Yes. One to carry you and me, and the other to carry Feodor and our luggage, together with the supplies we shall need for the journey. This is not England, you know, where an inn might be found almost anywhere along the route. We shall be travelling many miles through uninhabited terrain and it is important that we are prepared for all contingencies."

The morning was cold and clear, and the air stung her cheeks as Nikolai handed her into the sleigh. It was made of carved wood, painted crimson and decorated in gold leaf with a hood over the top to protect them from the weather. A leather apron was supplied which could be tied on if necessary across their legs for protection. Nikolai passed her a fur travelling rug to tuck around her knees and then climbed in beside her. The horses were fresh, and restless, their black satin coats gleaming darkly against the snow. The whip cracked and they were off, rattling across the wooden bridge that spanned the Nieven and out into the vastness of the snow-swept landscape beyond the town.

Despite the cold, Lucy felt exhilarated as snow crunched beneath their runners, and the horses blew plumes of steamy breath into the ice-sharp air. The day was crisp with expectation, sunshine bouncing dazzlingly off the snow, the trees motionless beneath their fairy-tale burden.

She glanced at Nikolai, but there was nothing in his expression to tell her whether he was sharing her own sense of adventure. His head was thrown back, his profile etched sharply against the white glare of the snow, the reins held carelessly in one hand. He looked aloof; a man whose heart was as icy as the Neva in mid-winter. Unconsciously Lucy sighed and glanced back to where Feodor was driving his team behind them.

It was mid-year before they entered the forest, which Nikolai told her was the home of the charcoal burners. He slowed the horses slightly to allow Feodor to pass them and explained to Lucy that Feodor would go on ahead so that he could have their meal waiting for them when they arrived at the posting inn where they were to spend the night.

"With any luck, tomorrow we could be in St. Petersburg. We shall stop now to have something to eat and stretch our legs, but don't wander too far," he warned her. "These forests are infested with wolves."

Lucy shuddered, glancing fearfully over her shoulder, as she stepped out of the sleigh.

It was strange how doing absolutely nothing at all could be so wearisome. Nikolai was extracting a basket from the back of the sleigh, and he handed her a chunk of rye bread and some cheese, smiling a little sardonically at her rather doubtful expression.

"My apologies if the cuisine is not up to English standards," he drawled mockingly, "but I think you will find it is better than nothing, and it will be nightfall before we stop again."

Lucy closed her eyes and took a tentative bite of the bread. Actually it was quite pleasant and so was the full, creamy cheese, but all she really wanted was a cup of fragrant, hot coffee. She noticed Nikolai was drinking something from a silver hip flask, but when he raised his eyebrows and proffered it to her, she shook her head.

"Very wise," he said dryly. "I do not think you would care for our national drink. I have some water if you are thirsty."

Lucy took it gratefully. She was beginning to understand what he meant when he said that travelling in Russia was a far more serious undertaking than travelling in England.

Within half an hour they were on their way again, sliding silently through a forest of silver birches, occasionally disturbing some small animal or putting up a flock of birds who had been searching for food.

The movement of the sleigh and the glare of the sun made her feel drowsy, and Lucy could feel her eyes closing as the sun started to dip toward the horizon, coloring the snow deep crimson. The landscape entranced her. She had never known such an air of stillness, almost of enchantment, a land waiting for the magician's wand to free it from its frozen captivity. Pools lay like polished mirrors fringed by ice-rimed ferns and grasses. Occasionally a sharp crack broke across the silence of the vastness, as a branch gave way under the weight of snow, dislodging a shower of white softness to fall into the deep blanket already covering the earth.

"It reminds me of the story about the Ice King," Lucy remarked sleepily, as they passed a herd of red deer. She hadn't realized she had spoken aloud until Nikolai glanced at her.

"Which story is that?"

It was a fairy-tale Nanny used to tell her and she was

45

embarrassed at being caught out in the childish indulgence of remembering it. "It is nothing really . . . . "

"Tell me," Nikolai insisted.

It had grown colder and heavy snow clouds were banked up against the horizon. Lucy shivered and pulled up the hood of her coat.

"It is about a King who lived many years ago," she began slowly. "He had everything he wanted, but he could take no pleasure in it because he did not have a heart. One day, when he was out hunting with his court, he met a magician, and he told this magician how much he longed to have a heart. For many years the magician had loved the Princess Odessa whose father's lands bordered the King's, but the Princess did not return his love, and so to punish her the magician put a spell on her that made her fall in love with the King.

"At the same time he granted the King a heart, but because he was a cruel, unkind, magician, the heart he gave the King was made of ice, so that the King could not return the Princess Odessa's love . . . Russia reminds me of the Ice King," she finished awkwardly. "That is all . . ." "That is all . . ."

"But you haven't told me the end of the story," Nikolai reminded her. "Presumably it does have a happy ending?"

There was a strange expression in his eyes. One Lucy was not sure that she liked. They were gleaming with an unfamiliar brilliance that she suspected was caused by some deep rooted anger.

"Well?" he commanded.

"It does have a happy ending," she agreed hesitantly, trying to avoid his eyes. "The Princess was so distressed that the King could not return her love that she cried for a week and a day, and in his cavern on the mountain the magician gloated. However, he had overlooked the power of love, for the warmth of the Princess Odessa's tears melted the ice heart the magician had given the King. As the ice melted the King's heart came to life and . . . ."

"Most affecting," Nikolai interrupted harshly. "If

your King had had any sense he would have kept his ice heart. Or better still, done without one altogether."

He sounded so angry that it was some time before Lucy dared to glance at him again. The afternoon was fading rapidly: snow flakes were starting to drift down from the leaden sky. The horses' pace had slackened perceptibly, and Lucy sensed that although Nikolai had said nothing, he was anxious about the deteriorating weather. They were deep in the forest now; and with the failing light, long shadows seemed to creep out of the trees, filling the silence with an almost menacing quality. Lucy shivered and burrowed deeper into her rugs. She was cold now that the sun had gone, and excitement had given way to a nervous fear. Even the horses seemed to be affected by the atmosphere; their ears twitching as though straining for sounds inaudible to the human ear.

It had started to snow very heavily, thick white flakes, driven by a wind that seemed to have sprung up out of nowhere coating the horses and the sleigh. Nikolai was concentrating all his attention on the animals. He glanced over his shoulder at Lucy.

"I don't want to risk stopping to put on the apron. Will you be all right?"

She nodded, not wishing to burden him further by letting him see how cold and frightened she was, sensing that the situation was more dangerous than he wanted her to know.

Night came with appalling swiftness: there were no stars, no moon, only the endless wind and driving snow, and the terrible, ceaseless cold that seemed to penetrate through to her bones.

When the sound came, sending a frisson of dread down her spine, it was almost a relief.

"Wolves," Nikolai shouted to her grimly, as he fought to control the panicking horses.

At home in Wiltshire Lucy had never dreamed that one day she would find herself fleeing across icy wastelands, pursued by a pack of wolves. It sounded like something out of one of Mrs. Radcliffe's novels, but it was real enough! The howls of the hungry animals grew louder by the second. The terrified horses were sawing on the reins, almost bolting in their panic to escape from the predators they feared more than any others.

Lucy closed her eyes and hung onto the side of the sleigh which was now rocking wildly from side to side, almost overturning as they left the road and plunged through the forest.

"What's happening?" Lucy gasped anxiously.

"I think there's a charcoal burners' hut in front of us." Nikolai gestured to the remains of some tree stumps. "They've obviously been working in this area recently. If we can find the hut we can stay there until morning. It will be safer than trying to outrun the wolf pack, especially with tired horses."

"But what about Feodor? Isn't he expecting us?"

"He'll be all right," came the laconic reply. "When he sees this storm he'll guess that we're sheltering somewhere, and he'll wait for us to catch up with him." He cursed as one of the horses stumbled, and then started to limp badly. He brought the animals to a halt and leapt down into the feather-soft snow, throwing the reins to Lucy.

"The snow has packed hard in his hoof. That's what's making him limp," he explained tersely when he came back. "I wish to God we could find this damned hut. Unless I do something about it quickly he'll go lame."

As he climbed back into the sleigh, Lucy saw a gray shape move in the trees.

She clutched instinctively at his arm. "Nikolai! Over there! I think I see the wolves."

"Where?" He searched the wood in the direction of her shaking finger, dexterously flicking the long whip over the horses' heads. "Hang on," he commanded grimly. "Let's hope the horses don't get the wolves's scent, otherwise I'll never be able to hold them!"

It seemed to Lucy that they travelled for hours over the rough ground, deeper, and deeper into the forest, the image of those sleek gray shapes, with their red eyes, lolling tongues, forever to the forefront of her mind, but in reality it could only have been minutes after Nikolai had examined the horse's foot, that they came upon the charcoal burners' huts in a small clearing.

Lucy was powerless to prevent a small sob of relief rising to her lips. Through the whirling snow she saw Nikolai's face, grim and set, as he brought the sleigh to a stop, and started to unharness the horses. Without a word, Lucy went to help him, knowing that this was not the time to play the helpless female. Her father's head groom had been as insistent that she learn to look after her mounts as her father had been that she ride them properly. Watching Nikolai out of the corner of her eye, she started to soothe the second animal, while he led the first into one of the larger huts. He came back and took the reins from her fingers.

"They'll be quite safe in there. I'll feed them and remove the snow from their pads. With any luck they should be fit enough to carry on in the morning."

She helped him carry the oats into the hut, unloading the rest of the sleigh while he attended to the horses. She had put everything in the next largest hut, choosing it merely for its size; but when Nikolai came in, he grunted in approval, as he saw the small stove in the middle of the floor, and the logs beside it.

"We're in luck," was his only comment. "The charcoal burners must have had to leave early because of the weather."

Lucy was surprised at the ease with which he lit the fire. Somehow or other she had imagined him scorning such homely tasks, but his movements had a deftness that plainly came from long practice.

There was some food left over from their lunch and he divided it scrupulously into two halves, passing one portion over to Lucy. There was nowhere to sit but the floor, but Nikolai had spread the fur rugs in front of the stove, and it was pleasant enough, if one contemplated the weather outside.

They ate hungrily in silence, each engrossed in private thoughts.

Nikolai found some tea on a shelf and managed to

make them a hot drink by melting down some snow and boiling it on the stove. Lucy sipped it gratefully, warming her hands on the cup from the wicker basket. The tea, having a strange flavor, seemed to burn its way down her throat, almost making her choke.

"Don't drink it too quickly," Nikolai warned her, with a wry smile. "I've added some Vodka to it. It will help you to sleep."

Lucy opened her mouth to protest, but she was already beginning to feel rather odd; almost lightheaded. Outside the wolves howled, but the sound barely impinged upon her. She felt lapped in a glorious warmth spreading like fire through her limbs and relaxing them from the tension of their flight through the forest.

"It's very pleasant," she said formally and politely, trying to focus on Nikolai's face, which seemed to be floating about in a most disconcerting fashion.

She saw the white flash of his teeth, in what was the nearest he had come to a smile while in her company.

"Don't get a taste for it," he advised her. "As it is, I think I've rather overdone it." He sighed, and seemed to be looking at her rather oddly. Lucy thought she heard him say, in an undertone, "Perhaps it's just as well," but she could not be sure.

When the "tea" was gone, Nikolai stoked up the fire. Outside the wind was keening bitterly, and Lucy snuggled down into her coat.

"We must try to get some sleep now," Nikolai said. He stood up, casting a long shadow across the room, and a shiver ran down Lucy's spine.

"We'll lie on one of the rugs and use the other two to cover us."

Lucy's head was spinning, as she stared rather owlishly at him, wishing he had not been quite so generous with his Vodka.

"We?" Was that squeaky, nervous voice really her own?

"That's right," Nikolai agreed neutrally. "It's an old Cossack trick. If the fire dies out in the night, we could freeze to death. Both of us need our sleep too much to stay awake tending it, even if the fuel would last that long. The warmth of our bodies will keep us both alive."

Lucy felt the color run up under her skin. Instinctively she clutched her coat to her, staring up at his motionless figure.

"You cannot be suggesting that I . . . that we . . ." she stammered painfully, until he cut her short by saying curtly,

"That we sleep together? I'm afraid I am, but let me assure you that you need have no fear for your virtue, if that's what is worrying you." He permitted himself a wry smile.

"In this instance your body is only of interest to me for the warmth it generates—nothing more!"

Lucy wanted to tell him that the thought that he might be attempting to seduce her had never crossed her mind—he was her cousin after all, but there was something as yet unawakened in her that shied away from the thought of such close contact with a man—any man, be he her cousin or anyone else. She was even tempted to confide her fears, but something in his expression stopped her. All at once she felt painfully shy.

"Now, if you have overcome your fit of missishness," he said evenly, "perhaps you will come and lie down here between me and the fire."

Bemused, she did as he bid, her eyes, did she but know it, round with apprehension, questioning him mutely as he removed his cloak with a brief shrug, placing it over her, before he lay down at her side. He then pulled the rugs around them both, rolling toward her until it would have taken only the slightest movement to bring her into contact with his body.

His breath stirred the ringlets at the back of her neck, and where previously she had been exhausted enough to sleep on her feet, now she was tiresomely alert, stiffening at every alien sound, as tense as a bow-string.

It seemed a long time before she heard the firm, even sound of Nikolai's breathing, telling her that he slept. Her own breath seemed to have gathered in a tight ball, somewhere in her chest. She dared not think what the aunts would say about her present situation. Nikolai was her cousin, she comforted herself, and knew the dangers of this arctic wilderness as she did not. Even so, it was a long time before her tired body started to relax.

As she lingered on the verge of sleep, Nikolai's voice reached her admonishingly through the darkness. "Lucy, if you don't go to sleep, I shall be obliged to get up and give you some more Vodka."

Outside a wolf howled and she trembled, suddenly glad of the reassuring warmth of Nikolai's body next to hers. She stopped trying to fight the urge to let sleep claim her, and as the logs burned down to orange embers, she started to relax against the solid comfort behind her.

She awoke toward dawn to find that she had turned over in her sleep and now lay with her head pillowed against Nikolai's shoulder, his arm curved around her waist. The fire had gone out and her breath formed clouds of vapor in the cold air. She shivered and Nikolai's arm tightened. He muttered something in his sleep, pulling her against him. There was a dark shadow along his jaw. In sleep he looked curiously vulnerable. She shivered again, telling herself that his reaction was merely instinctive. The pressure of his arm prevented her from moving. She was terrified he might wake up and find her in his arms. His face was only inches away from her own. As she tried to wriggle free, he bent his head, his lips suddenly fastening over her own, in brief, passionate demand.

For a timeless span of eternity Lucy lay frozen against him, hardly able to comprehend what was happening. The mouth that looked so hard, felt surprisingly gentle. Lucy had never been kissed before, and she was afraid of the feelings his caress aroused. Was this what the aunts had meant when they shook their heads and said she had inherited her mother's temperament?

Desperate to be free, she pulled away from the constraining arms, and in immediate retribution Nikolai's lips hardened, punishing her for her defiance. Her senses whirling, she called his name, protestingly. "Nikolai— please! It's me . . . . Lucy . . ."

Although his eyes remained closed, his arm slackened enough for her to pull away from him.

"Please God do not let him remember anything about this," she prayed as she tried to compose herself. That would be the final humiliation! She would not allow herself to wonder exactly of whom he had been dreaming!

It seemed that her prayer was to be granted. Seconds elapsed as she tried rather shakily to crawl out of the rugs and then some sixth sense made her look at Nikolai.

He was lying with his eyes open, watching her with a rather enigmatic expression. Hot color stormed up under her delicate skin.

"Did you sleep well?" she asked rather inanely.

"Very. Unlike you," was the dry response. "Did you know you talk in your sleep?"

Lucy shook her head, hoping her burning face would not give her away. Did he know that he kissed in his?

"It's dawn," she said, unnecessarily. "How long will it take us to catch up with Feodor?"

"Not long."

He stretched and pushed aside the rugs. "I'm afraid there isn't enough wood left to boil any water. You'll have to wash in what's left from last night. I'll go and see to the horses."

"What about the wolves?"

"They won't bother us during daylight, but I don't want to delay here any longer than we need."

They left before it was properly light, and with the horses fresh and rested, it didn't take them long to reach the inn and Feodor. He exclaimed sympathetically at Lucy's wan face, but when he suggested that she rest, Nikolai said grimly that he wanted to press on. Lucy dared not look at him. He had made no reference to that brief, urgent embrace, and was, hopefully, unaware of it, but that did not stop her own conscience berating her for allowing it, even though she was at a loss to understand how it could have been prevented.

By evening they had reached St. Petersburg. Lucy was ready to drop with exhaustion and so were the horses.

She was barely aware of reaching the city, of sweeping past elegant stucco buildings painted in a variety of pastel colors, or of the Neva, a frozen ribbon, glittering under the stars as they drove down Nevsky Prospect to stop outside the palace Prince Kuragin had had built when he was a young man.

The sleigh stopped, jolting Lucy out of her numbing tiredness. She stared up at the imposing height of the Palace. A feeling of nervous dread seized her in a paralyzing grip. The Palace was far grander than she had imagined, nothing like the buildings to which she was accustomed. Everything about the sugar-white edifice, decorated with baroque gold-leaf overwhelmed her. There was too much richness, too much grandeur . . .

Nikolai was waiting for her to alight. A flight of shallow steps leds up to the door. Someone had opened it, and light spilled out into the snowy street. As they entered the hallway Lucy caught her breath in mingled awe and dismay. Towering marble pillars seemed to rise endlessly before her bemused eyes. Stark white walls hung with rich tapestries in scarlet and gold, huge golden urns decorated with Eastern lavishness, gem-studded icons, all mingled dizzingly in front of her.

Another door opened. Two huge, leggy bundles of fur uncurled themselves and flew at Nikolai, barking and wagging feathery tails. The dogs were black with cream muzzles and feet.

"My borzois," Nikolai explained. "No need to be frightened. They are gentle creatures at heart. Come and be introduced to them . . ."

Even the dogs lacked the homeliness of papa's hounds, Lucy thought despairingly, watching the antics of Nikolai's elegant pets.

"Will someone stop those damned dogs barking," a voice cried gruffly from the stairs. "What the devil's going on."

Lucy's eyes fastened instantly on the figure on the stairs, her small face turned upwards, so that the light fell directly upon it.

"It's all right, grandpère," Nikolai replied.

"Nikolai! Is that you! Have you brought Lucy? Is she there?"

A firm hand gave her a small push toward the stairs. "Well, aren't you going to answer him? Or are you having second thoughts?" Nikolai mocked scornfully.

For a few seconds Lucy found it impossible to speak because of the lump in her throat.

"I'm here grandpère," she whispered rather shyly at last, staring up into the darkness.

The man who walked toward them limped slightly despite his proud bearing. He was quite different from Lucy's imagined picture of him; very like Nikolai, which for some reason she had not expected, only with snow-white hair where her cousin's was black. What really caught at her heart though, were the unmistakable marks of past sufferings clearly delineated on his face.

The old Prince looked down into the compassionate eyes of his granddaughter and held out his arms. Lucy flew into them, returning his kiss, laughing and crying at the same time as she struggled incoherently to bridge the gap of eighteen years in as many minutes.

At last the old Prince held her away from him, surreptitiously wiping away an errant tear.

"She is so very like my dearest Nadia," he said to Nikolai. "So very, very like. I only wish your father could have lived to see this day. He missed his sister and would have replied to her letters had I not forbidden it. Ah, what folly is pride. But we must not dwell on the past! You look tired Nikolai!"

"The weather was bad," Nikolai responded briefly as they embraced. But he made no mention of their flight from the wolves or the night they had spent in the charcoal burners' hut. There were still traces of tears on Lucy's cheeks. She tried to wipe them away without being seen, but Nikolai caught the gesture and a sardonic smile twisted his mouth. "Don't stop now! You have yet to cry all over Tante Sophy!"

"Nikolai!" the old Prince rebuked. "You are unkind. Wait until you are my age, then you will understand. Once I was like you and scorned human emotion, but I learned. Lucy, come and sit with me and tell me about your journey. You must be tired—poor child. The servants will bring you a cup of tea. Your Aunt Sophy is upstairs fussing over your room. She will be down shortly."

As he spoke he drew Lucy into a large salon furnished with a quantity of gilt chairs covered in straw satin. Matching fabric adorned the walls, toning with the richly woven rugs lying on the polished floor. The room was heated by an ornately enamelled stove, grander than the one she had seen in the inn, and there was a huge silver-gilt samovar on a small table in front of it, steaming gently as the servants made the tea. The furnishings were an entrancing mixture of East and West, so many strange, new things to catch Lucy's eye that she was content to look about her and let the conversation flow over her head.

Nikolai's voice jolted her rudely out of her reverie, and she realized that he and her grandfather were discussing papa. Her hands trembled indignantly as she remembered the insults of the woman at the inn. ". . . whatever the differences between Stanton and myself," she heard grandpère say, "in the end he proved himself generous by sending Lucy to me . . ."

"I dare say he didn't have much option," Nikolai commented dryly. "It was either you or a quartet of harpies . . . or at least that's what Vorontznov told me."

Lucy choked on her cup of tea.

"Nikolai is only teasing you, Lucy," her grandfather said kindly. "Naturally, your father preferred to entrust you into my keeping, as your nearest male relative, than into your aunts' although I understand their very natural concern for your well-being."

Lucy daren't look at Nikolai. She bit her lip as she remembered Aunt Jane's behavior on the day they met. One didn't need to be a mindreader to see that her aunt cared more for Lucy's vast fortune than her person.

"I had not realized your father was such a wealthy man," Grandpère continued. "We must take care to guard you from fortune hunters, little one. There are many in St. Petersburg who wear their fortunes on their backs. I shall instruct Nikolai to have a care for you in these matters. I do not get about as much as I used to, and there is no point in expecting Sophy to act as she ought." He shook his head indulgently. "You will like your aunt, but there is no denying that she is a feather-headed creature."

"Ivan Ivanovich," chimed a light, female voice. "How dare you say so? Nikolai, defend your poor old aunt, and tell your grandfather that he wrongs me!"

Sophy fluttered into the room reminding Lucy of a small, bright-eyed bird. She was dressed in the skimpiest of muslins, her person decorated with a good many items of jewelry, but despite her obvious love of ornamentation and high fashion, the smile she bestowed on Lucy, when she saw her, was both heart-warming and sincere.

"So this is Nadia's child! My dear girl!"

Lucy was embraced again, with far more fervor than she had ever known from her father's aunts. "Tante Sophy" as she was instructed to call her new relative was about Lucy's own height and despite the fact that Lucy knew she must be somewhere near her fiftieth year, she had a general air of sprightliness that somehow seemed to defy mere age. There was certainly none of the censorious disapproval about her Lucy had suffered so long from her paternal relatives. Indeed Tante Sophy made Lucy feel as though their roles were reversed and it was she, Lucy, who was the adult, and her aunt a charming, impulsive child.

She chattered non-stop in a confusion of half-finished

sentences, mostly about fashion and her plans to bring Lucy "out," pausing here and there to dart a look at the two men standing silently on the side-lines, before rushing on.

Unexpectedly, it was Nikolai who rescued Lucy.

"Your new-found niece is falling asleep where she stands, Tante. Let her rest before you start quizzing her about London fashions. If you will excuse me, Grand-père, I shall have to report to Alexander. The Regiment is on duty at the Winter Palace, and I was granted leave of absence only as a special favor."

"Yes, yes, of course. You must go. Lucy, come and bid your cousin, good-bye. How long shall you be at the Palace this time, Nikolai?"

He shrugged. "A matter of days only, no more."

"You will not forget about procuring an invitation for Lucy for the Grand Ball at the end of the month? She will be out of her first six months's mourning by then, n'est-ce pas?"

Lucy nodded, and as though he read her mind, Grandpère said gently, "Your father wrote me that you were not to mourn him Lucy. He knew how much you loved him, and he would not want you to hide your pretti-ness away in drab black garments."

Lucy forced a tremulous smile. "I know. He told me I was not to wear black."

"Black! Certainly not!" Tante Sophy exclaimed in shocked accents. "Tomorrow we shall go through your clothes. Petite, and then we shall see what you need. There will have to be a gown for the Ball, of course. It is the first of the season. All St. Petersburg will be there . . ."

". . . and already you are dreaming of our little Lucy taking them all by storm," Grandpère laughed. "And why not! She is a beauty, as her mother was before her!"

For a second tears dimmed the old eyes, but they were quickly gone.

Nikolai instructed Feodor to remove the dogs, who were clambering excitedly over his knees, sensing his im-minent departure. He stood to embrace his grandfather, then turned to Lucy, his hands gripping her shoulders.

Exhaustion lay in dark smudges under her eyes, and in the light of the candles they looked bruised violet instead of blue. To her surprise he kissed her lightly on both cheeks, as he had done Grandpère, and in growing silence Lucy realized that she was expected to return the embrace.

She did so, stiffly, self-consciously, aware of the mockery covered by his bland smile.

"Thank you for bringing me to St. Petersburg," she said politely, like a child at a party.

He paused by the door. "Don't thank me yet, cousin. Wait until you have had a proper taste of our way of life."

Once he had gone, the excitement which had sustained her through the proceeding hour fled, leaving her exhausted. She was only too willing to agree to Tante Sophy's suggestion that she retire to her room and soak in the hot bath the servants had prepared for her before going to bed.

Tante Sophy accompanied her to her room, which was charmingly decorated in pale lemon and white. There was a large portrait of a young girl above the fire, and Lucy had no difficulty in recognizing it as her mama.

She gave a cry of delight and ran forward to examine it. "Ivan Ivanovich had it hung there for you," Tante Sophy informed her. "Before, he had it in his own suite of rooms." She patted Lucy on the cheek. "You are a very good child and it will give him much happiness to have you here. Now . . ." she began briskly, as though half ashamed of her momentary emotion, "you must sleep. When you have had time to accustom yourself to our ways I shall introduce you to society."

Tante Sophy was not quite as feather-brained as she liked to pretend, Lucy thought drowsily as she submitted to the ministrations of the chattering maids. They spoke in Russian, and she wondered how long it would be before the language ceased to sound so foreign. Tucked up in bed, waiting for sleep to claim her, she had a sudden vivid memory of lying in Nikolai's arms. She closed her eyes, willing the thought to disappear, telling herself that from now on she must think only of the future.

Tante Sophy had the good sense not to force too many new experiences on her charge all at once. Lucy's first few days in Russia were spent in the confines of the Kuragin palace getting to know the servants, drinking endless cups of tea from the ever-bubbling samovar and enjoying cosy gossips with Tante Sophy.

She also spent a part of each day with her grandfather, both of them delighting in their new-found relationship. Grandpère had as caustic a tongue as his grandson, but in him it was tempered by old age's tolerance for human frailty, although Lucy suspected that that tolerance was hard-won. He told her much of her mother's childhood; the grandmother she had never known and the aunt and uncle.

"You must try to make allowances for Nikolai," he said one afternoon when they were sitting in the library, watching passers-by on the snowy streets. "He lost both his parents at an age when he needed them the most. Even now I don't care to remember it too much."

"What happened?" Lucy asked gently, sensing that he wished to tell her.

"A sleigh accident: their horses bolted and they were both killed. Nikolai was with them, but he was thrown clear. By the time the servants managed to catch up with the runaway sleigh they found him crouching by his mother, begging her to "wake up." He was twelve at the time. It was shortly after that that I heard your mother had died. I lost both my children within the same month."

Lucy's heart was racked with pity, both for her grandfather and Nikolai, but it was the picture of the small boy manfully trying to stem his tears, that lingered the longest.

"For a long time afterward, Nikolai suffered from terrible nightmares," Grandpère added soberly. "If he seems cold and hard, you must try to make allowances. I should like to see the two of you grow close."

Lucy saw no significance in the remark, but she noticed also that Tante Sophy seemed anxious that she and Nikolai should see more of each other.

"I shall be glad when Nikolai has completed this

period of duty," she confided to Lucy, one morning, as they drank their tea. "Then he will be free to escort you."

"And to prevent me from meeting any 'fortune hunters.'" Lucy commented humorously. "Grandpère says he owes it to my father to make sure that I am well protected."

"The best protection any woman can have is a husband," Tante Sophy said briskly. "But I don't think Ivan Ivanovich is anxious to lose you—not when he has only just found you!"

"And I am not anxious to lose him," Lucy said firmly. For some reason Tante Sophy's remark had alarmed her. She wanted to marry, of course, but not yet. Not until she could find a man who she could love as her mother had loved her father.

When a week had passed without any sign of Nikolai, Tante Sophy began to fret, wondering aloud why he did not call. As Lucy was beginning to learn for herself, her grandfather was frailer than he liked to admit, and depended on his grandson, not just for male company, but for help in running the vast Kuragin estates, and all manner of other matters as well.

"He will come as soon as he is able," the old Prince said placidly in response to Tante Sophy's anxiety. "I expect the Regiment keeps him busy."

At the very moment they were discussing him, Nikolai was seated in the Tsar's private sanctum, watching the Emperor of all Russia, across the desk. On it lay the reports he had brought back from England.

"So, it is definite then," the Tsar said at last. Physically he was as tall as Nikolai, but not as lean, with fair hair, and a handsome, if slightly morose face. "Bonaparte intends to invade us."

"He thinks of us as a plum ripe for the picking," Nikolai replied. Although the Tsar did not like to be reminded of the crushing defeat his army had suffered at Napoleon's hands, he considered Nikolai Kuragin one of his most able and promising colonels. For his bravery in the past he had awarded him the Cross of Saint Andrew. Now he frowned and looked at him across the table.

"What do you suggest, Nikolai?"

"As I see it, we have very little choice. We must either sue for peace or lure him into a false sense of security. If we could destroy that monumental sense of self-satisfaction which makes his Grande Armee the best in the world, then . . . perhaps . . . we shall have a chance."

"A small task indeed," the Tsar sighed. Thrusting his hands in his pockets he stared out of the window. "I am being pressed to sue for peace, Nikolai. There are those who would murder me as they murdered my father. I have no sons to come after me, but I do have two greedy brothers."

"I cannot advise you which course to take, Sire," Nikolai said quietly and respectfully. "Bonaparte wants Russia—let Russia show him that she does not share his desire. It is winter now. If Bonaparte intends to invade, he will wait for spring, to give him the good months for his campaign. An army such as his lives off the land it invades, but if there were to be no food . . . no fuel . . . if his victory should be delayed and winter should come . . ."

The Tsar swung around, the impatience fading from his face. "Of course! Why didn't I think of that!" He rang a bell on his desk and when an aide appeared he spoke to him: "Have General Kutuzov sent to me." When the man had gone he smiled rather wryly. "Kutuzov and I have never seen eye to eye, but he and Bagration are the best commanders we have. Very well. Let Bonaparte do his worst! I shall be ready! Russia will be ready!"

A tap on the door signalled that the audience was over, but as Nikolai rose, the Tsar stopped him.

"I have not yet congratulated you on being reunited with your cousin. You will, of course, present her to me at the Grand Ball?"

"She will be honored," Nikolai responded formally.

The Tsar smiled. "Not if she is anything like you, my friend. By the way, a word of warning. A certain gentleman whom I know you have good cause not to love, is back in St. Petersburg. You may recall that some time ago I gave an order that anyone found dueling would be banished to his country estates? That edict still holds good, Nikolai." He glanced at the scar on the other man's face. "The past is dead, Nikolai, and none can alter it. It is wrong to try."

"By the way," he announced, changing the subject, "I trust I can rely upon you to maintain the honor of the Regiment and win the Troika Race again this year?"

"I hope so too. I'm just on my way to the stables to find out if my horses have been properly cared for in my absence. Young Desilov, my second-in-command, promised he would have a care for them for me."

"You can tell him for me that he will lose his coronetcy if he has not," the Tsar joked. "A fine thing if you lost the trophy to the Hussars!"

Smiling, Nikolai agreed, but his thoughts were not really on the annual Troika Race along the frozen Neva. Instead, he was thinking about their earlier conversation and praying that Russia would prove strong enough to withstand the might of the French Army. The Tsar's other comment he ignored, although he fingered his scar once or twice as he hurried to the barracks. So Vasili Orlov was in St. Petersburg. Well, they would meet soon enough, and when they did ... his hand went automatically to the hilt of his dress sword.

At the end of her first week in St. Petersburg, Tante Sophy decided that Lucy was rested enough to go on a shopping spree. It was the first time Lucy had travelled by troika, a fast sled pulled by three horses, and she found the experience both novel and hair-raising.

Seeing it for the first time in daylight, she could understand why St. Petersburg was called the "Venice of the North." Even in mid-winter the light had a rare clarity, and she caught her breath in a gasp of pleasure as they criss-crossed the city's many canals, now frozen slips of silver in the pale sunshine.

They drove through a large square, dominated by a statute of Peter the Great, past the elegant edifice of the

Winter Palace, down along Nevsky Prospect. The crisp air rang to the tune of sleigh bells, people gathering in the wrought-iron shelters dotted along the carriageway, to warm their hands against the glowing braziers. Vendors selling piping-hot blinis, cried their wares in harsh, gutteral voices, and again Lucy was aware of an air of tense expectancy in the atmosphere. When she commented upon it, Tante Sophy agreed.

"That *is* St. Petersburg. In Moscow it is quite different as you will see when Ivan Ivanovich retires to his estates in the summer."

They turned off the main street into the shop-lined Morskaya, where troikas battled to get past one another, and ladies and gentlemen stood in small groups on the flagway inspecting the contents of the windows.

Lucy found the variety of available goods staggering. In the modiste's her eyes widened in pleasure at the bolts of silks, batistes, figured muslins, and cobwebby lace that were brought forward for her inspection. They far exceeded anything she had seen in London.

Tante Sophy was delighted by her reaction. "You haven't seen anything yet," she promised as she leaned forward to murmur an instruction to the modiste. Ten minutes later Lucy was gasping anew with pleasure at the beauty of the fabrics they were being shown. "I knew you would like them," Tante Sophy exclaimed complacently, fingering a roll of fine crimson silk embroidered with silver stars. She held up a bolt of jade green fabric woven with threads that ran through it like liquid fire.

"These are from the East," she told a bemused Lucy. "From far across the steppes and the markets of Eastern Russia!"

"They suit the young Barina's dark coloring," the modiste approved. "They are not the fabrics for a blonde or for a woman with less than perfect skin."

She held a bolt of midnight blue chiffon against Lucy's face to illustrate her point. In the mirror Lucy saw her own reflection; her skin as pale as the snow against the rich fabric, the intensity of the color, deepening her eyes to match it.

"Is it perhaps a little ... flamboyant?" Lucy asked uncertainly, releasing the fabric with regretful fingers. She couldn't forget the aunts' derogatory remarks about her mama, and she had no wish to make enemies for herself amongst the young ladies she would meet by dressing herself in a manner calculated to draw attention to herself.

"For a Kuragin, *nothing* is too flamboyant," Tante Sophy said with a trace of hauteur, adding more kindly, "These are the colors and fabrics of your ancestors, Lucy, but I forget the English side of you, and if you would prefer something a little more European?"

"No ... no ..." Lucy denied hurriedly, before she could change her mind. "I shall be guided by you Tante Sophy. I love the fabrics, truly I do ..."

It took them the rest of the afternoon to make their final choice, and in the end it was arranged that not only would Lucy have half a dozen morning dresses in embroidered muslin, a carriage gown in deep red velvet, and a dozen afternoon gowns in a variety of colors and fabrics, but also three ball gowns from the rich, Eastern fabrics Tante Sophy had chosen for her. The midnight blue was a must of course, for it enhanced her eyes, but she must have also the crimson and the jade, both so perfect for her coloring. In the end, since Lucy could not make up her mind between them, Tante Sophy had settled the matter by saying that she must have both. Lucy had never known shopping could be such fun.

Tante Sophy instructed their driver to take them back along Nevsky Prospect. Seeing several groups of skaters on the river reminded her that they still had to get skates for Lucy. While she was debating whether they should return to the shops or leave it until the morrow, another troika drew up, and its occupant hailed them.

A pretty, sprightly brunette climbed out, wearing a carriage dress of palest blue trimmed with ermine. She smiled at Lucy and dropped Tante Sophy a curtsey.

"Surely you remember me, Duchess? Last summer ... in Moscow ... Countess Morovskaya?"

"Er, yes, of course," Tante Sophy responded in a somewhat flustered fashion.

"And this, of course, must be Prince Kuragin's grand-daughter?" the other continued gaily. "How I have longed to meet her. All St. Petersburg is wild with curiosity. Will you not introduce us?"

Was it merely Lucy's imagination, or did Tante Sophy seem rather reluctant to comply with Countess Morovskaya's request? Certainly the Countess seemed to find nothing amiss in Tante Sophy's behavior.

"I am sure we shall soon be the best of friends, Miss Stanton," she declared vivaciously, "or may I call you 'Lucy'?"

Lucy had little option but to agree. The Countess was perhaps half a dozen years her elder, and while Lucy was flattered by her interest, it struck her that the other girl's manner was a trifle girlish for a married lady.

"You will call me 'Anna,' won't you?" she pressed a bemused Lucy, rushing on. "Will the Grand Duchess not permit us to walk a little way down the carriageway together so that we may get to know each other better? I swear I have been horribly lonely in St. Petersburg since my dearest Lucien returned to his Regiment."

Lucy did not know quite what to say to all this. She was beginning to find the Countess's manner rather over-whelming although it was impossible not to like the older girl.

"Very well. But do not walk too far, Lucy," Tante Sophy warned. "I shall wait here for you. I see an old friend across the road." Her manner was cooler than Lucy had been used to, and again she had the impression that, for some reason, Tante Sophy was not altogether pleased about their meeting with the Countess Morov-skaya.

However, no sooner had she stepped down from the troika than the other girl tucked her arm through Lucy's drawing her away.

"How fortunate that I should have come upon you in this manner. You will perhaps think it presumptuous of me, but from the moment I heard of your arrival I knew I should have to seek you out and warn you!"

"Warn me?" Lucy was startled, but before she could

question the Countess further, she continued seriously, "I discussed it all with my dearest Vasili—that is my brother, you must know—and he was of the same mind as myself. Distasteful though it might be, I could not allow you to step unprepared into the danger that awaits you!"

"Danger?" Lucy was becoming more bewildered by the second. They had nearly reached the end of the carriageway. Soon they would have to turn back to where Tante Sophy was waiting.

"Please . . ." Lucy begged. "I do not understand."

The Countess looked rather uncomfortable, and wrung her hands. "If only my dearest Vasili could have been with me. You will think me the vainest creature alive . . ."

Lucy was beginning to feel faintly exasperated by the Countess's vague manner. Why on earth had she sought her out in this fashion? It passed all comprehension. Plainly the other girl was in the grip of some powerful emotion. At length she pronounced dramatically, "There is no help for it! I shall have to tell you! I have heard that you are a great heiress, and I must warn you against your cousin, Nikolai Kuragin. He will propose a match between the two of you—this I am sure of. He has long looked for a wife who can match him in fortune and birth, and who better than his own cousin? You may be sure that the old Prince will support him in this decision, but I beg you, if you have any care for your future happiness—do not accept him!"

Lucy was appalled. "My cousin . . . you . . . but no, I cannot believe it . . ." she said slowly. "Why, he holds me in the greatest aversion . . ."

"That would not stop him," the Countess cried impetuously. "Believe me, I know what he is capable of. That monstrous pride of his admits no view but his own." She had recourse to a tiny lace-edged handkerchief. "There was a time when a match was proposed between your cousin and myself. Please do not think I speak from chagrin or jealousy; my dearest Lucien is the kindest husband on earth. In fact . . ."

There was a tiny pause which Lucy hardly noticed. She was too busy struggling to comprehend the enormity of what the Countess was saying. Now, comments which she had taken for mere inconsequentialities took on a new and disturbing meaning. Was this why Tante Sophy was so anxious for Nikolai to return from duty? She shivered suddenly, unaware of how pale she had gone, or how distraught she looked.

"In fact . . ." the Countess continued, "it was I who drew back from the match. Indeed I could not have done otherwise, even had I wanted to marry your cousin—not once I knew . . . that is . . . my dear Lucy, I hope you will not take this amiss, but your cousin . . . . Well I'm afraid there is no polite way of putting it. There was a servant girl from the estates near Moscow. She came to St. Petersburg last winter. Of course, one accepts . . . that is . . . ."

She was trying desperately to avoid Lucy's eyes, and Lucy herself was beginning to feel that she did not wish to hear any more. However, the Countess seemed unaware of her feelings, for she finished with a rush: "It was said that there was to be a child and that your cousin had cast her out. There was the most dreadful scandal, and when my brother accused him of acting in a less than gentlemanly fashion, they fought. You must have seen Nikolai's scar? It was said at the time that only the Tsar's high regard for Nikolai saved him from banishment. Personally I don't know how he can bring himself to show his face in St. Petersburg now . . ." She gave a rather petulant shrug. "Of course, that pride of his protects him from public opinion, but I could not bear for you to be deceived by him as I was. Naturally, my family would not even consider the match when his disgraceful behavior was made public, but who is there to protect you? I hope you will forgive me for telling you all this. Had your circumstances been different . . . but then Nikolai has always been a favorite with the Grand Duchess."

She hinted also that Tante Sophy would probably not tell her of the events of the previous winter.

"I warn you only so that you can be on your guard."

The Countess added, "And I hope you will forgive my presumption and that we can become friends."

They were approaching the troika, and Lucy made some mechanical response. Her mind felt numb, incapable of comprehending what she had just been told.

"I'm grateful to you, Countess," she said in a husky whisper, as they parted.

The countess smiled deprecatingly. "Someone had to tell you, and most of St. Petersburg stands in such awe of the Kuragin's that they would never do so. Indeed, most of them would think your marriage to your cousin a very fine thing, and then laugh at you behind your back when they talked about the old scandal."

Lucy caught her breath a little at this cruelty, but she knew instinctively that the Countess spoke the truth. Happiness was not the criteria by which the world judged a good marriage. Wealth, position, these were what mattered, and marriage to Nikolai would provide her with both.

But she was not going to marry him. As she climbed into the troika, her mouth set in a determined line. Papa would never have wanted such a marriage for her, and even if it meant defying Grandpère, she was not going to marry Nikolai!

Five

Time flew, and the first six months of Lucy's mourning drew to an end. Nikolai was on duty over Christmas; and partially because of this, and partially out of respect for Lucy's papa, the household at the Kuragin Palace spent the holiday very quietly indeed. Lucy attended church with Tante Sophy—so very different from Stanton Lacey's small Norman building, and afterward there were small gifts to be exchanged—nothing very lavish. Expensive presents, Tante Sophy confided, were saved for one's "name-day."

As January came in with fresh falls of snow, all Tante Sophy could talk about was the coming ball. It was to be the highlight of the season. All St. Petersburg was attending, but with Countess Morovskaya's strange warning and Grandpère's very evident desire that she should shine above all others, Lucy was quite dreading the occasion.

Tante Sophy, looking extremely fine herself, came to supervise the final touches to Lucy's attire. She was seated before her mirror wearing only her chemise while Tante Sophy's maid dressed her hair. She had piled the dusky ringlets on top of Lucy's head and was securing them with a small pearl bandeau, when Tante Sophy shook her head slightly, and instructed her to help Lucy into her gown.

It was lying on the bed, a pool of deep blue raw silk, the silver embroidery shimmering under the lights. As the

71

girl slipped it over Lucy's head and started to fasten it, Lucy could not help noticing how the color of the gown emphasized the unusual shade of her eyes, and how white her arms and shoulders appeared as they rose from the tightly fitting bodice. The skirts floated delicately when she moved, the loose panels giving her the appearance of some fragile, ethereal creature who might disappear at the first puff of wind. She might indeed have been one of the beautiful sprites said to inhabit the silver-birch woods and deep pools, a creature whose beauty was not of this world and who drew men on to their doom.

Tante Sophy and the maid studied her critically.

"It is exactly as I hoped." Tante Sophy approved. "Now run downstairs and show your grandfather. He is waiting for you in the library."

Lucy caught sight of herself unexpectedly in the full length mirror as she left the room and stared at her unfamiliar reflection. Was that really her image? That almost spiritual looking creature with the huge sapphire eyes and slender body?

"You will be the belle of the evening, there can be no doubt," Tante Sophy assured her. "Now hurry. Don't keep your grandfather waiting!"

Lucy knocked at the library door and entered rather timidly, suddenly shy. Her grandfather sat before the fire, looking very fine in his evening clothes. He gazed at her for a very long time.

"Lucy, tonight I am glad I am not twenty years younger, for you would surely break my heart ..." His eyes twinkled as he spoke, and Lucy sensed that for this evening he was determined to forget that other girl whom she so resembled and not let the past spoil his pleasure in the present.

"Come here," he commanded. "I have a gift for you. It was your mama's."

He took a box from the mantelpiece and opened it. Lucy stared transfixed as he lifted from it a collar of gold set with huge sapphires. That the jewelry was very old she did not doubt; it was almost paganly barbaric in its beauty, and she shivered a little as the cold metal touched her skin.

"Grandpère, it's beautiful," she said softly.

"But not as beautiful as you, my child. It has been in our family for hundreds of years. I had hoped to see Nikolai's bride wearing it before now, but it was not to be."

The hairs on Lucy's neck stood on end. Was Grandpère going to tell her that he wished *her* to be that bride? Apparently not. He was removing something else from the mantel. A comb in the same design as the necklace and Lucy guessed that he and Tante Sophy had planned this surprise together. The sapphires complemented her gown exactly, but it was on her prettily flushed face and glowing eyes that the old Prince's own eyes lingered, not upon the fortune she wore around her neck. He took her in his arms and kissed her solemnly on both cheeks.

"May your life bring you every happiness little one."

"Thank you, Grandpère." Her voice was tremulous, her eyes going instinctively to the gilt framed mirror on the wall, where the reflection of the necklace flashed and glittered with the uneven rise and fall of her breathing.

"Are you two not ready yet?" Tante Sophy scolded, entering the room. "Lucy, petite, the necklace is perfect. Have you the comb? Maria can finish your hair now."

She was on her way downstairs, her tongue caught between her teeth as she concentrated on keeping her skirts off the stairs, when Lucy realized there was someone approaching the house. The borzois's ecstatic barks warned her who it was long before the door opened; and when Nikolai walked in, she was standing nervously on the stairs. In the distance she could hear Tante Sophy chivvying the maids and Grandpère's deep, soothing response, but in the hall there was no sound at all. Even the dogs had fallen silent, their feathery tails motionless, as they sensed the hostility in the atmosphere.

Nikolai wore the white and gold dress uniform of his Regiment, a scarlet, fur-lined cloak, unfastened over it.

He presented an impressive picture, Lucy admitted reluctantly, but there was no warmth in the smile he gave her. All at once the Countess's warnings came crowding back into her mind. As Nikolai advanced toward the stairs, she shrank back slightly, unaware of how wide and frightened her eyes were, until his own narrowed gaze warned her how much she was giving herself away.

His teeth flashed in a dangerously mocking smile and as he stood looking up at her, Lucy's heart began to pound with heavy, uneven beats. Quite what would have happened she did not know, for at that precise moment Tante Sophy saw her nephew and came hurrying down the stairs. "Nikolai! My dear boy! How handsome you look. What a picture the two of you will make. Why I dare swear St. Petersburg has not seen such a handsome gentleman since your grandfather was a young man!" She bustled about, handing Lucy a wrap and commanding a servant to remove the dogs whose spirits had made a recovery and who were capering about the hall, barking. "Come along. We don't want to be late. Lucy will ride with you Nikolai, I will follow with your grandfather."

All St. Petersburg seemed to be abroad. The night air rang to the sound of sleigh bells, and the stars shimmered every bit as brightly as the embroidery on Lucy's gown as the troika swished over the frozen snow. It was a night of fairy-tale enchantment; everything still under its coating of frost, silvered by the light of the full moon shining down on them, but Lucy could not enjoy the ride. She was too nervous, too conscious of Nikolai sitting next to her and the speculative look he had given her as he handed her into the troika. She was not silly enough to imagine he cherished any tender feelings for her—far from it, but she was beginning to realize in what great affection he held their grandfather. Should grandpère favor a match between them . . . she shivered and tried not to let her thoughts dwell on such an unhappy subject. In many ways she wished the Countess had never spoken to her, had never enlightened her about her cousin's past. It was impossible to look at him—an arrestingly handsome figure

74

in his immaculate uniform—without picturing that poor peasant girl.

"Lucy!" Her cousin broke into her reverie. "Dreaming of the young men who will be swept off their feet by your beauty, not to say your considerable fortune?" he asked. "We're here. Come on . . ." His smile was cruelly sardonic, but there was no time to deny his assertions. They were out of the troika, joining the other guests streaming toward the entrance to the Winter Palace.

When they entered the ballroom, Lucy was impressed by the impressive malachite columns soaring upward to support the arched ceiling above their heads. Never had Lucy dreamed of such richness. Everywhere was jade and malachite, embellished with quantities of gold leaf. The Kuragin Palace was an impressive building, but it could not compare with this.

The ballroom was even more magnificent, with a lavish display of opulent luxury that quite took Lucy's breath away. But it was the dark green malachite columns, so polished, so cold, the color of Nikolai's eyes to which her gaze kept returning.

"It *is* very fine, isn't it?" Tante Sophy commented complacently, misreading her expression. "See, here comes the Tsar!"

The gold doors at the far end of the room opened slowly and the musicians began to play the first notes of a Polonaise. The Tsar wore a uniform like Nikolai's and Lucy's eyes went instinctively to her cousin, standing silently at her side. On his breast the Cross of Saint Andrew glittered ice cold as the frost-rimed Neva outside. He inclined his head slightly, as though aware of her covert regard and Lucy flushed, looking hurriedly away.

The strains of the music increased in volume. The Tsar was not hurrying. He paused occasionally to address some remark to his attendants and the woman at his side.

"Is that the Tsarina?" Lucy whispered to Tante Sophy, but it was Nikolai who answered her, his mouth compressing.

"No, that is not Elizabeth Alexeievna," he said curtly, "she is the Tsar's sister, the Grand Duchess Catherine."

The Tsar murmured to his sister, who laughed and made some reply, and brother and sister began to dance, gracefully circling the floor.

"That is the signal for others to commence dancing," Nikolai informed Lucy, placing a hand on her waist.

He hadn't asked if she *wanted* to dance, Lucy thought indignantly as he swept her onto the floor.

He was an excellent dancer, though; and to Lucy, who had seldom danced with anyone save her cousins' husbands, and cronies of her papa's, the experience was a revelation. Never had she imagined dancing could be such a pleasurable, heady affair. She even forgot that the arms that held her belonged to her detested, disgraced cousin, and she felt quite disappointed when at last the music stopped.

Prompted by Tante Sophy, Nikolai introduced her to a dozen or more of his fellow officers, who were all flatteringly eager to fill up her dance card. Lucy had a sensible head on her shoulders however. Delightful though the prettily extravagant compliments might be, they were not meant to be taken seriously, and while one young Captain likened her eyes to sapphires set in snow and another said she danced as gracefully as thistledown, she did not allow their praises to go to her head.

After supper, which she had taken with Tante Sophy and grandpère, refusing all the pleas of her would-be escorts to allow them to take her to the supper rooms, Nikolai approached her again.

He had been talking to several other gentlemen, none of whom seemed inclined to join their fellows on the floor. Their expressions hinted at matters of a more serious nature, and Lucy wondered about the subect of their conversation. However, she had no intention of questioning Nikolai.

"The Tsar has requested me to present you to him," he informed her in a cool voice.

Lucy glanced helplessly at Tante Sophy, wishing she could be assured that her curls were not tangled, or her cheeks over-flushed from her exertions on the dance floor.

"Go with Nikolai, Tante Sophy urged her.

Nikolai placed her gloved hand on his arm and led her across the polished floor. Lucy knew that a good many pairs of eyes followed their progress.

"That was a clever touch—dining with Grandpère," he remarked sardonically. "You have twisted him around your finger faster than I thought."

"I ate with Grandpère because I love him," Lucy replied stormily.

How dare he insinuate that there could be another—less honorable—motive for her behavior?

His smile derided her flushed cheeks and stormy eyes; and to her own consternation, it was Lucy's eyes that fell first.

The Tsar was sitting with his attendants. He rose when they approached and gave Lucy a charming smile. "So, this is your cousin, Nikolai." He raised Lucy's fingers to his lips, with another dazzling smile, before introducing her to his sister.

The Grand Duchess was a vivacious brunette about Lucy's own age and plainly not particularly interested in her own sex for she gave Lucy only the briefest of smiles, concentrating instead on the man who was standing behind her.

"You have not yet asked me to dance, Nikolai Andreyevich," she chided playfully.

"Because I could not get near enough to solicit your hand," Nikolai responded with unexpected gallantry.

The Grand Duchess dimpled a smile at him. "There is no one here now, but ourselves," she pointed out.

Nikolai smiled, and one of the Tsar's aides stepped forward to take Lucy's hand. He was a fresh-faced young man, plainly very much in awe of the Tsar, and nowhere near as excellent a dancing partner as her cousin, Lucy soon discovered. He trod on her gown, and to her dismay she felt the hem tear slightly. Across the other side of the room, the Grand Duchess was laughing up into Nikolai's face. Lucy was glad when the music stopped and she was free to leave the floor. She found Tante Sophy and explained about her gown, before retiring to the salon set aside for the use of the ladies to see what could be done about her torn flounce.

The salon was decorated in shades of peach and white. Several ladies stood in front of the silver-gilt mirrors, and a maid came forward to ask how she might aid Lucy. They examined the tear together, and found it not as serious as Lucy had first feared. In no time at all the maid was able to mend it with tiny, invisible stitches.

On leaving the salon, Lucy felt a hand on her arm.

"My dear Lucy. I thought it was you! Did you tear your dress? Such a shame. It is quite the loveliest in the room. I confess to being exceedingly jealous!"

It was Countess Morovskaya. Lucy gave her a rather hesitant smile.

"Thank you, Countess . . ."

"Anna, please! Did we not agree that we should be friends? Come, let me introduce you to my brother, Vasili. From the first moment he set eyes upon you, he has been pleading with me for an introduction. I do declare that had I not chanced upon you leaving the salon, I should have been obliged to approach you in the ballroom or suffer my brother's displeasure for many weeks to come!"

Lucy could not help laughing. Anna had such a droll way of talking that it was impossible not to like her.

Count Vasili Orlov was just as charming as his sister. Like Nikolai he was in uniform, except that Nikolai's uniform was white with gold trimmings, Vasili Orlov's was dark blue with crimson facings. The differences were soon explained. Vasili was in the Hussars, and Nikolai, as Lucy already knew, belonged to the Tsar's own personal regiment.

Soon Lucy was laughing helplessly at Vasili's teasing compliments. If only this boyish young man could have been her cousin, she thought wistfully. Perhaps he wasn't as arrogantly handsome as Nikolai, having mid-brown hair and quite ordinary hazel eyes, but his nature was so much gentler, so much more attuned to her own.

They were waltzing when he raised the subject which had made his sister seek Lucy out several weeks before, apologizing beforehand for his mention of it; "I couldn't help noticing that Kuragin introduced you to the Tsar. Has there been any mention of the matter my sister discussed with you? I ask because I am concerned for you. When my sister told me how pretty you were, I confess I did not believe her. Now, I know she understated the description." He saw Lucy's expression and hesitated. "But perhaps I am wrong? Perhaps you do not find the thought of your cousin paying his addresses to you disasteful?"

Lucy gave a faint shake of her head. Truth to tell she could think of nothing *more* distasteful, but there were some things that should not be discussed outside one's family, however tempted one might be.

"I hope I am not wrong," Vasili added softly, "I should hate to lose you to your cousin, so shortly after making your acquaintance—an acquaintance I am not ashamed to admit I hope might ripen in time to something . . . deeper?"

There was a question in the words, but Lucy chose to ignore it, and Vasili did not embarrass her by reverting to the subject. Instead, he drew her attention to Nikolai, who was still dancing with the Grand Duchess.

"You know, of course, that to introduce an unattached young lady to the Tsar, is tantamount to seeking his approval to a betrothal?" he commented.

Lucy's shocked face gave him his answer, and he smiled grimly. "Typical of Kuragin. No doubt he hopes to force you into a position where you cannot refuse him. I know my sister has told you of . . . of certain matters, I cannot bring myself to repeat in the presence of a lady. Should you question him, he will deny it, of course. That is his way. His pride will admit no wrong, but you may be sure that Anna and I will stand your friends." He released her as the music ended and escorted her back to Tante Sophy, who smiled rather vaguely and continued her conversation with another turbanned dowager.

Perturbed and upset, Lucy was so engrossed in her

thoughts that she did not see Nikolai approach until he was standing in front of her. Was it her imagination, or was his stance as intimidating as it appeared? His eyes looked like pieces of frozen jade in the cold haughtiness of his face. She had never been more afraid of him, and her hand shook as he drew her to her feet.

They had barely waltzed more than half a dozen steps when he said curtly, "You were dancing with Vasili Orlov. Who introduced you?"

Lucy's eyes flew to his face, as though by doing so they could divine his thoughts. "His sister, the Countess, Tante Sophy introduced us and..."

"...and the Countess takes it upon herself to find dancing partners for you, is that what you would have me believe?" His lip curled disdainfully. "A Kuragin has no need of the endeavors of an Orlov."

He swept Lucy expertly into the curve, his face grimly remote. Lucy felt sure he must hear the suffocating beat of her heart.

"You were conversing with Orlov for a considerable time. What was he saying to you?"

Lucy's pulse gave a frightened bound. Her lips felt stiff and wooden. Her hand shook as she tried to think of something to say, but it was useless. She could not bring herself to lie.

"He said he had seen you introducing me to the Tsar." It was the truth, but she hoped he would not question her further. Her hopes died when she saw the expression on his face.

"And?" he queried softly.

Lucy felt like a hunted animal. There was no way of escape, save for pulling herself free of Nikolai's constraining arm, and fleeing the floor, and that she most certainly could not do!

"He... that is... they..." She was stammering hopelessly, but those hard green eyes would not let her escape. They followed every betraying gesture, iced with determination.

"They wanted to warn me that you might be con-

80

sidering a match between us," she said at last in a low voice. "I know about what happened last winter, Nikolai, about the ... scandal and ..." She stopped, appalled by the look of grim fury on his face. The hand on her waist had tightened so much she feared that she would be bruised black and blue by morning. "He will deny it." Vasili had warned her, and she was very much afraid he was going to be proved right.

"I am obliged to Orlov for his interference," Nikolai ground out, when he had control of himself. "In the event, it is wasted, for I have not the slightest intention of making you an offer."

"I knew you did not have any tendre for me," Lucy felt obliged to say, "but the ... that is ... I think Grand-père would like the match ..."

Green eyes bored mercilessly into her. "You think me the sort of man to marry at another's bidding?"

It wasn't what Lucy had meant at all. What she had thought was that his obvious affection for the older man might have constrained him to make a marriage that would find favor in the eyes of his grandfather. But it was too late to say so. Nikolai's face was as white as his uniform, a look of blind rage in his eyes.

"I suppose it never occurred to question Orlov's motives for repeating these 'rumors,' or to doubt the truth of them?"

Lucy's expression gave her away.

"So. You judged and found me guilty! Well, it is not for me to seek to change that judgment. Believe what you will, but know this. No son of mine will ever have a mother who bears him out of duty, and scorns his father in the secret corners of her mind. If Vasili Orlov is what you want, I wish you joy of him, but be warned: Grand-père will never countenance a match of that order, as he will tell you soon enough himself. Orlov has run through his own fortune and no doubt already anticipates yours, but, of course, you are foolish, and will believe whatever tale he spins you, as I now know."

The music had stopped without her aware of it.

Nikolai turned abruptly and left her, striding through the crowd that parted then swallowed him up. Shaken, Lucy grappled to understand the intensity of his anger.

"You have already judged me," he had said, and wasn't there a grain of truth in the accusation? And yet, Vasili had been so sincere, so convincingly concerned, unlike Nikolai who had unleashed his anger on her without a second thought.

Even in his fury Nikolai had made no attempt to deny Vasili's accusations. Surely that must prove something? Besides, what reason could there possibly be for the brother and sister to accuse him of so dreadful a crime if it were not true? And then there was that telltale scar, gained in his duel with Vasili. And yet she could still feel the heat of Nikolai's scorn. At least she need have no fear of a proposal from that direction now!

Toward the end of the evening Anna approached her again.

"Has Nikolai made you a declaration?" she asked conspiratorially. "I saw him dancing with you." She pulled an expressive face. "I did not envy you—he looked so grimly furious! I know him well in that mood. His pride is twice that of any other man!"

"I think you must have been mistaken," Lucy said gently. "I do not believe it is his intention to make me an offer." She could not confide in a conversation to the other girl, but she felt impelled to disabuse her of her suspicions concerning a marriage between Nikolai and herself. She could not bear to face her cousin's fury if it became common knowledge in St. Petersburg that he was expected to marry her!

The enjoyment had gone out of the evening. Her feet ached in the flimsy sandals: she was tired and longed for her bed. Tante Sophy recognizing the signs of exhaustion drew her to one side, suggesting that they prepare to depart. Grandpère was conversing with a fierce-looking gentleman in a general's uniform, but he seemed very pleased to see them and interrupted his conversation to introduce Lucy.

The general smiled genially and announced that

Lucy was the prettiest young lady he had seen in quite a long time. Lucy was too tired to be properly appreciative of the compliment, but she managed a very neat curtsey and when she rose from it, Nikolai was walking purposefully toward them. Lucy saw with appalled horror that his eyes were stilled iced with held-in anger.

He paused for a moment to acknowledge an acquaintance and Lucy realized that Vasili Orlov was standing right behind him. Vasili moved, his dress sword brushing against Nikolai's arm. For a second the two men faced one another, frozen in a small tableau.

There was an infinitesimal pause as though others remembered the events of the previous winter, and then Vasili was smiling cooly at Nikolai, the tilt of his head challenging as they measured one another across the silence.

Lucy clutched her hands, holding her breath. "Please, God, don't let them quarrel," she prayed desperately.

Vasili was first to speak. "I hear that you are hoping to win the Troika race for the fourth year in succession next month, Prince. The Hussars have elected me as their challenger. How do you feel about the two of us making the odds more interesting? Ten thousand kopecks says you cannot win again this year!"

There was an expectant hush among the onlookers. Lucy bit her lip. How foolishly brave of Vasili to challenge Nikolai so openly.

"If you wish to throw away your money, who am I to stop you?" Nikolai sounded bored, indifferent almost.

Lucy expelled her breath on a sigh of relief, not quite sure what she had been expecting. Someone clapped Vasili on the back and called him a fool for venturing so much against Nikolai's fabled horses, and the tension diffused like mist in the sunshine.

At the end of the evening Nikolai accompanied Lucy and Sophy to the waiting troikas, solicitous for their comfort, but when Lucy expected him to take his place next to her he stood back saying instead, that he had business with the Tsar which precluded him from joining them. For Lucy's ear alone he added coldly, "I trust I have now relieved you of the anxiety of worrying about whether I might decide to make love to you on the way home. Let me assure you, cousin Lucy, the day I do that, I shall either be drunk or mad." And with that cruel jibe he swung around on his heel, disappearing into the yawning darkness of the room beyond.

"Did you enjoy yourself, petite?" Tante Sophy asked kindly, patting Lucy's hand. "I know you won't take this amiss, child, but you would be wise not to pay too much attention to Vasili Orlov."

"Because Vasili has no fortune to speak of, or because his sister was once betrothed to Nikolai? Oh yes, I know all about it, Tante Sophy, Anna herself has told me!"

Tante Sophy looked distressed. "Promise me you will say nothing to Nikolai? On that particular subject he is very sensitive."

With good reason, Lucy thought grimly,

"I'm surprised that Vasili Orlov dares to face Nikolai so openly after the events of last winter." Tante Sophy continued: "That young man is riding for a fall, you mark my words!"

In the gold and green ballroom, Vasili Orlov smiled condescendingly at the man standing in front of him, his eyes resting on the scarred face for the merest fraction of a second.

"I'm afraid I cannot comply with your request, Prince," he drawled lightly. "Your cousin is an enchanting creature and it is my hope that our friendship will flourish." His smile mocked openly now. "My sister tells me she was excessively shocked when she learned of your own less than gentlemanly behavior. How often I have heard it said that pride goes before a fall, but I have never seen the proverb more graphically illustrated than tonight." He bowed, the light shining on his bare head. "Until our next meeting, Prince. To the victor the spoils eh? I have a feeling that you are not destined to win the Troika Race this year."

As he turned to walk away, Nikolai said softly. "You haven't won yet, Orlov."

"Nikolai?"

He hadn't heard the Tsar approach. Together they watched Vasili Orlov's dark blue uniformed back disappear into the crowd. "Remember what I told you," the Tsar warned. "I want no repetition of last winter's affair. Then I was prepared to let you off lightly, another time I would not feel so generously disposed. Now, come and dance with Catherine, and then we shall discuss the latest news from France. By the way, what were you saying to Orlov?"

"I was telling him that if he hopes to recover his waning fortunes via my cousin, he is doomed to disappointment."

The Tsar gave him a sideways glance, started to speak, and then thought better of it when he saw the expression in his companion's eyes.

Six

The troika race was to be held at the end of February and was, as grandpère explained to Lucy, a much looked forward to event. They were sitting in the library, Lucy on the floor, her head resting against grandpère's knee's as she listened to him describing his own youth, and the fun they used to have.

"We were not so sophisticated then as you are now. Nor did we have the threat of war hanging over us." He stifled a small sigh and Lucy felt a pang of guilt. Poor grandpère! He had already lost his son and daughter and now he must face the threat of losing his beloved grandson as well. Lucy had learned enough from their conversations to know that if Bonaparte declared war on Russia, Nikolai's regiment would be in the forefront of the ensuing battle.

Lucy had not seen Nikolai since the night of the Tsar's ball. She suspected he was avoiding her deliberately, and she did not know whether to be relieved or sorry. She tried to reassure herself that she was not to blame if he chose to take offense because she knew of his past indiscretions, but she could not forget the white fury on his face when he stood over her on the ballroom floor. She wished with all her heart that Vasili had not offered Nikolai that additional challenge. There had been something so implacable on the older man's face, that she feared for the outcome should Vasili be the victor—not, according to grandpère, that there was much chance of that happening! Nikolai's Arabs were the finest horses in all Russia; fleet as the West Wind, and added to that there was no driver anywhere to compare with Nikolai for skill. Lucy was not reassured. From the moment in the ballroom, when Vasili challenged Nikolai, she had been conscious of a sense of deep forboding which not even the arrival of the rest of her new gowns had been able to alleviate.

On several occasions since the ball, Tante Sophy had mentioned Anna and her brother. Lucy suspected, although Tante Sophy was too easy-going to say so, that her aunt did not approve of the growing friendship which had sprung up between the trio—more than mere friendship in the case of Vasili, Lucy had to admit if she was honest. Although never stepping beyond the boundaries of convention, Vasili had, nonetheless, made it very clear how he felt about her.

Seated beside grandpère and Tante Sophy on their way to the troika race, Lucy reflected that whatever her own doubts on the subject of the race, these were obviously not shared by the rest of St. Petersburg.

Nevsky Prospect was crowded with brightly painted troikas and sightseers, all intent on enjoying the occasion. In fact the road was so busy that it was quite some time before the troika could set them down. Several persons stopped to converse with them, all offering their good wishes for another win for Nikolai.

"He will win. Just you wait and see." Tante Sophy whispered to Lucy. "The Tsar himself is coming to watch. It is the honor of his regiment that Nikolai upholds."

A huge carnival sprawled across the Neva in a confused jumble of stalls, tents and humanity. The cries of the stallholders mingled with those of the skaters whom Lucy was watching enviously. Rich Eastern perfumes scented the air. A group of guards clustered around a stand selling freshly made blinis, laughing and eating. Next to them was another stall piled high with dishes of sour cucumbers, rolled herrings in soured cream, and chunks of rye bread. Lucy's mouth watered. Huge braziers burned under flimsy wooden shelters, the smell of hot coffee enticingly fragrant. Gilded, fur-lined sleds jostled with down-at-heel droshkies, their drivers clustered together over one of the braziers. It reminded Lucy vaguely of York Fair, only on a much larger scale. While Feodor forced a way through the crowd for them, Lucy watched a juggler swallowing fire, and a troupe of cossacks smoking pipes. Beside them, their strange draggle-tailed little ponies nudged their pockets looking for tid-bits.

An acquaintance of Tante Sophy's bustled up to them, her sharp eyes speculative.

"My dear Sophy," she breathed. "So exciting! No one has ever won the race four times running!"

"Meaning that she doesn't believe Nikolai can, I suppose!" Tante Sophy commented tartly when she had gone. "Odious creature. I never liked her anyway!"

"Come along Sophy," the old Prince instructed. "Nikolai will be waiting for us. Lucy will want to see his horses, and if we don't hurry we shall be too late. The race will have started."

Lucy's breath caught in her throat. If only she could think of a reason for avoiding the coming confrontation. She had no desire at all to see Nikolai, and she suspected it was a view he would more than likely share.

The crowd parted obligingly to make way for them. Lucy heard someone remark, "Look! There's the Tsar, and Count Sperinski is with him!" She turned her own head, straining for a glimpse of the Tsar and his portly Prime Minister.

Several of the less important races had already been run, but there was no doubt as to what was to be the main event of the day. Betting had been extremely heavy, so Feodor told them as he came up to lead them to Nikolai. "But my master will win!" he predicted confidently.

Grandpère gave a faint smile, but Lucy could tell he was worried. She thought of her cousin's proud, angry face and what it would do to him to lose publicly to Vasili and felt a renewal of her earlier misgivings.

When they eventually reached Nikolai he was standing talking to a fellow officer. A young lieutenant was holding his horses's heads. He blushed when he saw Lucy, and she recognized him from the Tsar's Ball. Just as she smiled in acknowledgement of his greeting, Nikolai turned, and Lucy felt the color seeping into her own face.

"Grandpère!" He embraced the older man and then both of them turned toward the horses, engrossed in a purely male conversation which left Lucy free to glance around her. A small group several yards away caught her attention. Vasili and several other young men in Hussars's uniforms. Anna was with them, and she raised her hand in greeting. Lucy responded, aware as she did so that Nikolai was watching her. A shaft of sunlight glittered on his gold epaulets, blinding her for a second.

"The others are waiting for you to wish me well," he told her curtly. "That is, of course, when you are able to remove your attention from Orlov."

"The others?" Lucy looked around, ignoring his latter remark. Grandpère gave her an expectant smile, and her heart sank. Standing on tip-toe she touched Nikolai's cold cheek with her lips. His hands steadied her, warm through the crimson carriage dress she was wearing.

"You will never make an actress! Now come and be introduced to the horses. Grandpère expects it," he warned her harshly, as she started to pull away.

The Arabs tossed their heads, arching their glossy necks, pirouetting prettily on dainty hooves. Lucy held her breath, lifting a cautious hand to stroke the nearest velvet muzzle.

"They won't eat you, you know," Nikolai murmured sarcastically at her side.

Their coats were as black as night, and they looked like animals out of a fable, all fire and grace. They were harnessed abreast in the Russian fashion, the two outside horses fastened loosely at either side of the shafts with only the leader standing firmly between them. Lucy closed her eyes and then looked again. A man would need to be an expert driver indeed to manage three horses such as these and in such conditions. The Arabs snorted as though agreeing. Their traces were white leather studded with silver, and small, chiming bells that rang out melodiously every time the animals moved. The sled was scarlet and so fragile that it frightened Lucy to look at it. And it was to these frail structures and their own skills that Nikolai and Vasili must entrust their lives. Across the ice Lucy's eyes met Vasili's and she made a silent prayer that both men would survive without injury. Whatever she personally thought of Nikolai, he was her cousin, her grandfather's heir, the last of a long, proud line, and she could not bear to see him meet his death for the sake of a silver trophy.

The starting pistol cracked out across the crystal air. The two teams surged forward, Nikolai's blacks and Vasili's chestnuts. The Arabs were as fleet as morning stealing across the sky, and neck and neck with them were Vasili's chestnuts. English horseflesh at its best.

No one could doubt that the teams were well matched. Grandpère was concentrating on the race, his eyes darkening a little as he studied the two teams.

"Orlov didn't have that team last year," he muttered to Lucy. "I suppose that doting sister of his bought them for him. A pity. He'll ruin them within twelve months. The man doesn't know how to treat decent horseflesh."

At his side Lucy smiled, without lifting her eyes from the two tiny sleds. Dear grandpère. Under that fierce air he assumed, he doted on Nikolai as much as Anna did upon her brother.

At the turn the two teams were still neck and neck. Lucy was standing on tip-toe, craning over the heads of the crowd to try to get a better glimpse, caught up in the general excitement despite herself. In front of her a group of Hussars were cheering themselves hoarse and she heard one of them say, "Orlov might just do it!"

"He'll have to," one of his companions agreed dryly. "They say he's put his last kopeck on this race!"

Poor Vasili! Lucy bit her lips. Was it very disloyal of her to hope that he might win? It was not that she wanted to see her cousin defeated, more that she could not bear to think of Vasili in straitened circumstances because of his impulsive wager. Illogically she blamed Nikolai for this. Had he wanted to she was sure he could have prevented Vasili from making the bet.

Vasili's whip whistled through the air with a harsh whine catching the leading chestnut on the flanks.

"Damn fool thing to do." Grandpère growled. "He'll never catch Nikolai using a whip like that. Kindness works better than curses. We have a saying in this country 'why beat a woman when she will please you better with kisses!' "

Tante Sophy remonstrated with him, but Lucy noticed that his eyes twinkled a little as he watched her digest his remark. All she could assume was that Nikolai was far fonder of his horses than he was of his women!

At the second turn Nikolai was leading by no more than a hair's breadth. There was a flurry of snow and ice as the fragile sled slewed into the corner. Lucy closed her eyes. When she opened them again both teams were safely round. Grandpère took her arm.

"Come, we shall get a better view a little further down."

They found a spot three or four yards away from the Tsar and his retinue.

As they came thundering down the straight, Nikolai was in the lead. Lucy was torn between relief and sorrow —relief because she feared for the outcome were Nikolai to lose, and sorrow because of her personal preference for Vasili Orlov. As they came toward them, the Arabs seemed to be breathing fire, their breath hanging misty-white on the coldness of the afternoon. Behind Nikolai, Lucy saw Vasili raise his whip, and the chestnuts surged forward, their muscles straining in the effort to get past the Arabs. Lucy held her breath. Such a short distance between them! She closed her eyes unable to look, and heard the whip crack through the air again, followed by angry roars. Her eyes flew open. The Arabs were half a length in front of the Chestnuts. Grandpère's hands were clenched angrily on his stick.

"What happened?"

"Orlov whipped Nikolai's horses."

"It must have been an accident," Lucy protested. "They were so close together!"

Her grandfather made no response. He was concentrating on the drama being played out in front of them. Tension hung on the air as intangible as the particles of frost, but there, nonetheless. The two teams were so close together that it was impossible to see who was in the lead.

Then it happened.

One moment Nikolai was leaning forward to urge his team on, the next Vasili's whip snaked out, catching him on the wrist. Lucy could not believe the action was deliberate. The two teams were so close together that it would have been almost impossible for Vasili to avoid catching Nikolai, but plainly Grandpère did not share her view. His face was suffused with anger.

"Just what one might expect from an Orlov," he muttered under his breath. "Upstarts, the whole damned lot of them."

The chestnuts had drawn level with the Arabs. While Lucy held her breath they started inching forward, and she saw that Nikolai had transferred the reins to his left hand. There was barely half a mile to go.

Suddenly a small child shot out of the crowd right in front of Nikolai's Arabs.

The crowd gasped and Lucy closed her eyes, convinced that Nikolai would be forced to let his horses trample the small body.

"Dear God!" she heard grandpère cry, and she looked up to see Nikolai swinging his horses around in front of Vasili, leaving the child unhurt. Someone retrieved him from the ice. The Arabs, wild-eyed and foam-flecked were charging toward Vasili's Chestnuts. With every second Lucy expected to hear the high-pitched scream of injured horses as the two teams collided. Grandpère had gone pale, all his attention concentrated on Nikolai. Lucy knew what he was thinking. Was he to lose his grandson in the same way he had lost his son? Her own small hand reached out and covered his. Their eyes met.

"He will be all right Grandpère," she comforted, hoping that it might be so.

"I pray so child. . . ."

Suddenly there was an excited roar from the crowd in front of them.

"He has done it. Nikolai has won!" Tante Sophy cried triumphantly. "He managed to pull his team clear, and he has beaten Orlov. Lucy, quickly, run down and congratulate him. We shall follow you. Go now!"

Reluctantly, Lucy did as she was bid. The Tsar was already congratulating Nikolai and she hung back, wishing Tante Sophy and grandpère had not lagged behind. Not a half dozen yards away she could see Vasili surrounded by his friends. He looked so dejected that her heart went out to him. After a glance at Nikolai, to assure herself that he was still deeply engrossed in conversation with the Tsar, Lucy slipped across to Vasili.

He welcomed her with a rueful smile. "Your cousin runs a hard race."

"But you did very well," she consoled him. "I'm sorry you lost though. If that child had not run out! What could have possessed him?"

"*I* do not know. Unlike your cousin. He has already as good as accused me of engineering the whole incident to make him lose!"

He shrugged aside Lucy's shocked "Oh no, he cannot have done so!" and said soberly, I am afraid you are too charitable, where your cousin is concerned. Your grandfather has arrived. I think he is looking for you. Dare I hope that our friendship will still continue?" he asked ruefully. "After this I shall be as near a pauper as makes no difference, but I can still take you skating or for a sled ride . . . provided they allow me to keep my horses."

Still burning with indignation on Vasili's behalf, Lucy was only too ready to do anything which would show Nikolai just where her sympathies lay; and before they parted, she had agreed that Vasili might take her skating, when an opportunity arose.

The crowd surrounding Nikolai melted away as Lucy

approached, and they were left facing one another. She gave him her congratulations in a rather stilted fashion, adding unconvincingly, "I am glad you won."

"Don't strain my credulity too much," she was advised. "I saw you commiserating with Orlov. Or were the two of you planning another attempt on my life. Perhaps he wishes to make sure of grandpère's fortune along with your own? I understand he has been given six months to pay off his creditors, otherwise he faces banishment. In my opinion the Tsar has been too generous, but then Orlov's sister is a very beautiful woman!" His mouth twisted bitterly as he spoke, but Lucy was too outraged to notice.

"An attempt on your life? What are you talking about?"

"Don't pretend you don't know. That 'child' who so conveniently flung himself under my horses and then disappeared without trace. Did you honestly think that was an *accident?*"

"It was!" Lucy burst out passionately. "Vasili could have been killed just as easily as you!"

Feodor had gone to the horses's heads and was walking them up and down. Grandpère and Tante Sophy seemed to have disappeared and they were quite alone.

"You would leap to Orlov's defense," Nikolai sneered. "Well you may as well forget about him. Grandpère will never allow you to marry him. He's a ruined man, who cannot even pay his debts!"

"Meaning the money he owes you, I suppose," Lucy said hotly. "If you had any real compassion, any feelings at all, you would release him from the obligation. I think I hate you Nikolai," she cried suddenly, quivering with a rage she could not wholly understand. "You are hard . . . and cold . . ."

"Enough!" he commanded peremptorily. "I have listened to enough. If Vasili Orlov was a man of honor he would never have entered into a wager he could not meet, but I don't expect *you* to understand *that*. So you hate me! Well in that case, cousin, allow me to give you something to hate me for!"

She was imprisoned in his arms; the Cross of Saint Andrew he wore on his chest, scratching her face as he grasped her chin and forced it upward.

"Nikolai!" Her furious protest was ignored. His mouth came down on the softness of hers, fierce and hard, as it conveyed his searing anger, draining her of all ability to think or feel.

"There—now hate me all you will!" Nikolai released her abruptly, stepping back, leaving her to raise trembling fingers to her quivering, bruised mouth. Tears weren't very far away, but her own anger, growing to match her cousin's, kept them at bay. Pride would not allow her to betray herself into weakness before this man! Eyes dark and stormy with resentment clashed with another pair, cold and remote as the ice-encrusted North Sea.

"You will cease this friendship with Orlov," Nikolai said coldly. "Do you understand?"

Never. Never! The words rose on a sob but were never uttered. "The day I make love to you I shall be either drunk or mad," he had said to her not so very long ago. But then what had just passed between them had not been an act of love, but one of hate!

Tante Sophy bustled up to them, frowning a little as she glanced from Nikolai's shuttered face to Lucy's pale one.

"You gave us all a terrible fright, Nikolai," she scolded. "That wretched child! What could his mother have been thinking of! Will you be coming back with us?"

"I think not!"

How cool and controlled he was, Lucy thought bitterly watching him walk away, but he will not dictate to me, I shall make my friends where I choose!

The outcome of the troika race was a nine-day wonder, but Lucy did not weaken in her resolve to pursue her friendship with Vasili Orlov in defiance of Nikolai's command; and she availed herself of every invitation he extended to her.

He took her riding in his sleigh, chaperoned by Anna. They walked by the Neva. He invited her to watch a parade of the Hussars on the Field of Mars, and they met constantly at the many balls she attended in company with Tante Sophy.

On the day she was engaged to go skating on the Neva with him, Tante Sophy raised her eyebrows a little. "Again? My dear, don't you think you're rather overdoing it?"

Lucy pretended not to understand. Tante Sophy was far from being the empty-headed creature she portrayed. Lucy suspected that she had guessed that her continued friendship with Vasili owed as much to a desire to defy Nikolai as any wish to further the acquaintance.

She went in to see her grandfather before going out. He was beginning to look very frail, and Lucy sensed that his health was not as good as he liked to pretend. He asked her where she was going but made no comment when she told him, and she kissed him gratefully as she left. Dear grandpère! He at least seemed to accept that she was perfectly capable of making her own decisions.

The stall-holders on the Neva were forecasting an early Spring. Lucy met Anna and Vasili by the bridge over the Fontanka Canal and sat down while her maid helped her on with her skates.

Vasili and Anna wer both excellent skaters. Her own skill was negligible in comparison.

"Let Vasili show you," Anna coaxed. "He is a marvelous partner."

She was quite right. With Vasili's arm supporting her Lucy found she was able to manage the most complicated of movements. Breathless from her exertions she allowed Vasili to sweep her into a mock waltz, unaware that he was leading her away from the other skaters, until he brought her to a standstill in the shadow of the bridge.

"Dearest . . . dearest Lucy," he murmured unsteadily. "Tell me you are not entirely indifferent to me."

Sensing that he intended to embrace her, Lucy moved away. The hazel eyes narrowed slightly, but apart from that he made no attempt to constrain her.

"Perhaps I mistake the matter and you are just

96

amusing yourself with me while you wait for your cousin to come to the point," he exclaimed bitterly. "After all, I have nothing to recommend me. No fortune; nothing but an unsullied name . . ."

"Vasili please!" Lucy could not bear to hear the unhappiness in his voice. "It has nothing to do with Nikolai. You should not be speaking to me like this . . . I . . . we hardly know each other!"

"I'm sorry. Please forgive me!" He caught her hand, squeezing her fingers anxiously. "I forget how very young and untried you are. You go to my head like gypsy music, little Lucy, do you know that? Soon my regiment goes on maneuvers; will you miss me?"

Relieved that the conversation was flowing in less serious channels Lucy gave him a tentative smile. "Yes . . . yes, I shall. We have had a lot of fun together the three of us . . ."

Her eyes pleaded with him to understand that friendship was all she wanted, for the time being at least.

"And we shall have more," Vasili promised her. "Now I had better take you back to Anna before she starts chiding me."

The awkward moment had gone. Lucy let him take her hand and lead her back to where Anna was sitting waiting for them. Just for a moment she thought brother and sister exchanged looks, but the impression was gone almost before she had time to grasp it.

On the way back to the Palace, Anna chatted brightly in her normal fashion, pausing once to remark on an acquaintance they passed, but Lucy paid scant attention. What would have happened if she hadn't drawn away from Vasili? Would he have kissed her? Perhaps she should have let him. The embrace would have been a pleasant antidote to Nikolai's cruel harshness. She compressed her lips and stared blindly into the street. Her cousin was at Gatchina. Grandpère grumbled that the regiment kept him busier than ever it had in the past, but Lucy was not deceived.

"Isn't that your cousin?" Anna's question arrested

her thoughts in mid-flight. Her heart bounded in fright. It was one thing to be brave in Nikolai's absence; it was quite another to defy him openly, flaunting her friendship with Vasili in front of his very eyes.

"He's gone," Anna reassured her, her eyes narrowing. "Has he really made no attempt to secure you for his wife? I cannot believe he would let such a chance slip through his fingers."

"He knows I would never agree to such a match," Lucy replied unwisely.

"He knows! So . . ." Anna teased speculatively. "He *did* propose a marriage then?"

Lucy had no wish to go into the details of her conversation with Nikolai on the subject of marriage, but she had to say something to stop Anna speculating.

"Nikolai wants to marry me as little as I want to marry him," she said firmly as she got out of the troika in front of the Palace. "And that is an end to the matter."

Tante Sophy was waiting for her in the hall, her face pale and anxious.

"Lucy! Thank goodness you're back. It is your grandfather! A stroke the doctor calls it. He has given instructions that he is to remain in bed for at least a month, and even after that he must continue to rest!"

At first Lucy was too shocked to make any response. Poor grandpère. While she had been out enjoying herself, he had been taken ill. Conscious-stricken she started to run up the stairs, but Tante Sophy stopped her. "No, no, child you cannot go to him now. He is sleeping. Later, you cannot see him. Fortunately, Nikolai was here with him when it happened and knew just what ought to be done. He has gone now to ask the Tsar to grant him special leave so that he may be on hand. I cannot think how we would go on without him!"

Lucy's heart sank even further. It seemed shockingly selfish to be thinking of her own affairs when poor grandpère lay ill, but she could not conceive anything worse than having Nikolai in the house, about to oversee her every move. The spark of rebellion lit by his authoritative

98

manner was fanned by her growing resentment. Well, she would not let him stop her doing just as she chose! And if she chose to see Vasili Orlov, then she would!

However, it was not Nikolai, or even Vasili, who concerned her now, but her grandfather. Berating herself for not being there when he was taken ill, Lucy wandered in and out of the salon, waiting for the doctor to return and tell her how the old Prince was.

The doctor was a short, tubby gentleman, somewhat incongruous in his fine, court clothes. Lucy hadn't realized that Nikolai had summoned the Tsar's own physician, and she listened respectfully as he explained the nature of her grandfather's illness.

"He has suffered from a weakness of the heart for some years. I suspect his present plight arises from many causes: your own arrival, the recent, much publicized troika race, the threat of war with France; all these impose a further strain on his already weakened constitution, but with rest, and care, he will live for many years yet."

He smiled at Lucy's radiant expression.

"He tells me that he is to retire to Moscow at the end of Spring. That will be a good thing. With the more sedate pace of life there he will make a further recovery."

"May I see him?" Lucy asked breathlessly.

"Not until I have done so," a new voice interrupted, as Nikolai strode in.

He greeted his aunt and the doctor, bestowing a reproving frown on Lucy before questioning the doctor about the condition of his patient. Having received much the same answers as Lucy, he accompanied the doctor upstairs to the old Prince's suite of rooms, leaving Lucy to stare disconsolately after them.

"They will send for you when the doctor has finished his examinations," Tante Sophy consoled her. "Gentlemen hate ladies to see them at anything less than their best." She patted Lucy's arm reassuringly. "Doctor Lieven is the best in all St. Petersburg. Your grandfather is in safe hands."

Ten minutes later the doctor reappeared—alone—

and told Lucy, with a smile, that the patient was much recovered and insistent on seeing her.

Nikolai was standing by the bed when Lucy went in. In his night-shirt, his silver-head lying against the pillow, grandpère seemed somehow to have shrunk, and Lucy's heart skipped a beat. She whispered his name, choking back a small sob, and his hand caught hold of hers.

"Poor child. Did I give you a fright?"

Lucy swallowed hard. It wasn't so very long ago since she had lost her papa, and now this! As though he read her mind, her grandfather smiled. "Nothing to worry about, Petite. I shall live to dangle your children upon my knee, eh, Nikolai?"

He looked at his grandson as he spoke, and Lucy saw, with a small stab of alarm, that Nikolai was frowning at her.

"You will be a good child and do as Nikolai tells you while I am laid up, won't you Lucy? He has been telling me that you are seeing Vasili Orlov. There can be no match for you in that direction. Promise me you will not even think of it?"

Lucy swallowed again, and tried to ignore Nikolai, stern and unyielding at her side.

"We are friends, Grandpère, nothing more," she palliated, refusing to meet Nikolai's sardonic gaze. "You must rest now. I shall come back later."

Nikolai accompanied her to the door, and to her surprise followed her through it, grasping her arm tightly.

"You are in my charge now, cousin, and I shall not be as lenient as our grandfather."

"You cannot tell me what to do," Lucy threw back furiously.

"No? You heard what grandpère said. Or do you care so little about him that you would defy him to continue your *friendship* with Orlov? Does he know that while he lay ill you were entertaining yourself in Orlov's company? Oh yes, I saw you. Did he kiss you, under the bridge?"

Hot color burned up under her skin.

"What's the matter? Do you feel guilty? Well you might. Well you might!"

"Why? At least Vasili wanted to kiss me because he likes me, not to . . . to inflict punishment upon me . . ."

"Meaning?" Nikolai said softly, but Lucy refused to be vanquished. Her chin tilted firmly, rebellion in her eyes.

"You know what I mean, cousin. I suppose I should be thankful that I am not a serving maid upon whom you could force your attentions without check!"

He released her instantly, striding away in the direction of his own room and leaving Lucy alone in the corridor.

Illogically she was filled with a sense of shame for her outburst, a wish that she had not uttered those last heated words. There was no need for her to lower herself to her cousin's level; she rebuked herself as she went to her own room. It would not happen again! But somehow whenever she was confronted with Nikolai her good resolutions seemed to melt away like snow in the summer sun.

Seven

"Lucy child! For Heaven's sake, you are wearing yourself out, not to mention the carpet!" Tante Sophy put down her sewing and examined her niece's wan complexion. "If you continue like this you will be the one who needs to be nursed back to health and Ivan Ivanovitch," she scolded. "Hasn't Doctor Lieven assured you that he is well on the way to recovery?"

Lucy smiled listlessly. It was true that the little doctor was well pleased with his patient's progress. A summer spent in the rejuvenating air of Moscow would complete the recovery he had assured the anxious household. Only Lucy seemed unable to share in the general good spirits pervading the house. The reason was not one she could share with anyone. She could not forget that grandpère had fallen ill while she had been out enjoying herself, nor could she forgive herself. So during the weeks of the old Prince's illness she had stayed within the bounds of the palace, retiring to her own room merely to sleep.

She hadn't even noticed that winter had given way to spring; that outside the Neva had melted and that spring flowers bloomed in the summer gardens. Tante Sophy gave an exasperated smile.

"There is no reason for you to remain constantly at Ivan's side, Petite. He would not care to see you so pale, isn't that so Nikolai?" she appealed, as the others entered the room.

Lucy refused to look at Nikolai. A truce had developed between them because of their mutual concern for their grandparent, but it did not extend beyond the mere formalities of convention, and certainly not to Tante Sophy's personal sitting room.

"Certainly I cannot see any need for Lucy to behave like an orphan at the Wailing Wall. Grandpère survived very well without her for eighteen years, and I cannot see that several hours without her company now would prove injurious to his health so long as those hours are not spent in the company of Vasili Orlov. His regiment is back from maneuvers and by all accounts, he's living on whatever he can scrounge from his friends—a pretty suitor you have picked for yourself!"

His scorn whipped Lucy's temper to breaking point: "There is no shame in poverty. I would rather have a poor man than one who ignores every dictate of compassion and honor to . . ." She remembered just in time that they were not alone. The green eyes had darkened to jade and behind her Lucy could hear Tante Sophy tutting in a placatory fashion.

"Than to what?" Nikolai asked harshly.

"Than to desert someone at a moment of greatest need." Lucy returned quietly.

He turned on his heel and left without another word. "Lucy, how could you?" Tante Sophy reproached. "Especially when he is under such a strain with Ivan, and the Tsar summoning him almost daily to the Winter Palace. What can be going on do you suppose?"

Lucy had even less idea than Tante Sophy, although Feodor had confided that there was growing concern that the French intended to invade Russia. Napoleon had called for a meeting between himself and Alexander to "resolve certain matters," and the command had gone out to the Russian armies to hold themselves in readiness for an invasion.

Lucy listened to Feodor's gossip with one ear, still smouldering with the aftermath of her anger. Nikolai had no right to speak so disparagingly about Vasili, especially when he himself. . . . But that she would not dwell upon.

Instead she would concentrate on aiding grandpère toward full recovery. In less than a month they would be leaving for the estate outside Moscow. Apparently Nikolai would not be able to accompany them, and for that reason, Lucy was looking forward to their departure.

It was in this mood of overt defiance that Anna Molovskaya caught Lucy when she called later in the afternoon. She kissed her on both cheeks and studied her pale complexion. "My poor Lucy," she cried sympathetically. "What a horrid time of it you have been having. Never mind, I am come to invite you to accompany me to a ball being held on the Kamenoy Island. You will love it. We eat outside al fresco and we shall dance all through the night." She laughed. "If one can call it 'night' for at at this time of the year it never goes properly dark, and the sky is still light when the sun rises. The Tsar himself will be there. The Kamenoy Island is one of his favorites. They say he met his Polish mistress Marie Narishkine there. I wonder what it is like to be mistress of the Tsar of all Russia?" she mused, ignoring Lucy's shocked protest. "You will come with me won't you? Vasili will be there. He is very much in love with you, Lucy," she said seriously.

Lucy was both embarrassed and perturbed. She knew that Vasili was attracted to her but . . . in love . . . fond of him though she was, there was not that degree of emotion which would cause her to want him as her husband, and if she was honest she knew she must admit that she was seeing him as much to defy Nikolai as for any other reason. The ball would give her an opportunity to hint him away as delicately as she could before his own affections were too seriously engaged. Much as she liked Anna she suspected she was given to a degree of exaggeration and encouraged Lucy to believe Vasili was in love with her as much for her own entertainment as from any real belief in the strength of his emotions.

Tante Sophy was quite happy to agree to the outing. There was no need for her to chaperone her niece she advised Lucy, not when she was being accompanied by the Countess, and besides it would be as well for one of them to remain at home. "You will love the island," she informed Lucy. "Many, many times have I visited it, and there is such a magical quality about watching the sun come up over the Neva when the sky is still alight from the previous day!" She did offer one word of warning though, seeking Lucy out when she was preparing for the evening.

At first Sophy was a little hesitant, praising the way the maid had arranged Lucy's ringlets, and then admiring the rich coloring of the jade green gown, before venturing on the matter that had brought her to her niece's room.

"I know you will not take this amiss, child. You and Nikolai do not always see eye to eye, and perhaps that is to be expected, but he has your best interests at heart." She fumbled a little with her lace fichu. "What I am trying to say is that where Vasili Orlov is concerned, you would do well to heed his advice Lucy, if only to save yourself a broken heart. Vasili is a charming young man, but he must have a rich wife and soon. The Orlov's are not renowned for their fidelity—one only has to look at his sister. I should not like to see you enter that sort of marriage, my dear. Be guided by Nikolai and be on your guard against Vasili Orlov."

She was so plainly anxious that Lucy was compelled to reassure her. "I like Vasili, but that is all. However, if I did love him, Tante, I would not let his lack of fortune come between us."

Relief and affection warred on the older woman's face. "Nikolai is right," she murmured. "You have a lot of your mother in you. Now let me look at your gown! It is lovely. And remember what we have just discussed!"

Lucy kissed her and ran downstairs. A carriage was waiting to take her to join the Orlovs.

Lucy found them standing with a group of courtiers waiting for the boats which were to convey them to the island. Anna kissed both cheeks, and Vasili did the same, his eyes glowing ardently when he looked at her.

"Never has Gatchina seemed such a Hell on earth, although had you been there, I have no doubt it would have been transformed instantly into Heaven!" His words

were for her alone, the touch of his hand on her arm
warning Lucy that she must make haste to advise him of
her own feelings. They were seated together in the boat,
but because of the crush of people, there was no opportunity for them to speak privately.

The island was everything Tante Sophy had promised.
Rhododendrons bloomed profusely in scarlet and pink
along the water's edge, their petals floating on the pale
green water. Liveried servants assisted them from the
boats and escorted them up winding steps through lush
green grass dotted with a variety of flowers. The northern
light had a pearlescent, glowing quality, like the inside of
a shell, and the air was as soft and clear as a delicate
wine.

A troupe of gypsy dancers and musicians who had
been hired for the evening were sitting in a grove
strumming and singing. The music had the same magical
throbbing quality Lucy remembered from the posting
house. Someone struck a plaintive chord, the sound shivering across her skin, raising the flesh in tiny goosebumps.

"You are cold," Vasili exclaimed solicitously. "Come
and sit down over here and I will fetch you something to
eat."

While he was gone Lucy watched the gypsy dancers
and listened to the music. The evening had a quality of
recklessness she had not been prepared for. She had
recognized several persons from the Tsar's ball, but where
there had been all formal decorum, here there was something almost abandoned in the air. One young lieutenant
was seated on the grass, his head pillowed on the knee of
his companion, a young and extremely beautiful girl. She
stroked his forehead, and Lucy looked away, her cheeks
burning. There had been something unconsciously intimate
in the gesture. There was no sign of Anna; she seemed to
have completely disappeared. Lucy blamed her own lack
of experience for her prudery, but the uncomfortable
feeling that neither the aunts nor Tante Sophy would have
approved of the free way in which some of the guests
were conducting themselves, lingered and would not be
banished.

When Vasili returned with two silk cushions and a servant bearing a tray of food, she automatically edged away from him. He noted the gesture, but he made no comment until they were alone and he had handed her one of the cushions.

"Have I done something to offend you?"

Lucy reassured him quickly.

"No, it is not that. It is just that . . ."

"You find our ways a little different from those in England?" he asked understandingly. "There is nothing to worry about. It is just the way our blood responds to the coming of summer. However, if you would prefer to return to St. Petersburg?"

Lucy wasn't quite sure what she wanted. She only knew that there was something in the atmosphere of the island that made her feel increasingly uncomfortable.

Vasili took her silence for consent.

"I must go and tell Anna that I am taking you home. Will you wait here for me? I shan't be very long."

He disappeared in the direction of the house, leaving Lucy alone with her thoughts. Truth to tell, she was not anxious to remain on the island. Since Vasili had disappeared the gypsy music had lost its haunting quality and become frankly sensual. Couples strolled past her, arm in arm, and the laughter had long since given way to a smothering silence.

Vasili was gone longer than she had anticipated, and when he did return, she sensed that he was somewhat preoccupied. He frowned a little as he drew her down a narrow flight of steps, cautioning her to mind her step.

There are usually boats moored just down here, if we can find one, it will save us having to walk back across the island."

Lucy was grateful to him for his perception, and stepped gladly into the small rowing boat he found moored to the jetty.

He rowed in silence for several minutes. Lucy glanced about her, trying to recognize landmarks from their outward journey: on one side of them, a small island, which had been no more that a mere bump on the horizon when they left seemed to be growing larger with every passing second.

"Vasili," she warned urgently, "I think we're going the wrong way."

Intent on rowing, her companion merely lifted his head to acknowledge her comment. The first faint flutterings of dismayed panic began to stir inside her. They seemed to be heading straight for the smaller island!

"Vasili! Where . . . ."

She got no further. The prow of the boat was crunching over shingle, signalling that they had reached the little island.

Vasili climbed out, leaving Lucy to stare after him in dismay.

"What are you doing?" she demanded.

"You wanted me to take you away, and so I have," came the laconic response.

"But not to here," Lucy protested. "I wanted to go back to St. Petersburg."

"And so we shall," Vasili agreed cordially. "Tomorrow morning, when you have promised to be my wife!"

Lucy couldn't believe her ears.

"I'm sorry it had to be this way," Vasili added in a voice that wasn't sorry at all. "But there was no other way. I was going to propose to you tonight anyway, but when I told Anna that you wanted to leave . . ."

"Anna! You mean she *knew* about this?" Lucy could hardly credit it. Had both Anna and Vasili run mad?

"I will not marry you, Vasili," she announced firmly from the boat. "You cannot make me."

"You think not? I cannot agree with you. When Prince Ivan learns that we have spent the night here together, he will be only too anxious to see us married, you wait and see. Now be a good girl and come over here. Or do I need to come and get you?"

Despite her brave words, Lucy shivered a little in nervous fear. What on earth was she to do? Vasili plainly meant every word he said.

The last few moments had successfully destroyed any illusions she might have cherished concerning the sincerity of Vasili's feelings for her. Had he truly cared about her, he would never have subjected her to such base behavior.

Numbly she stepped out of the boat, scarcely heeding the water soaking into the hem of her skirt. The island was little more than a mound of rock and totally devoid of habitation apart from an ornamental summer house built in the style of a Greek temple.

It was to this building that Vasili took her, propelling her firmly in front of him.

"I will never marry you, Vasili," she reiterated as he set her free.

"Never?" he laughed mirthlessly. "Oh, I think you will," he said softly. "I will give you an hour to think over what I have said. If, at the end of that time, I find you have not come to see reason, I shall be obliged to take steps that will render our marriage, not only necessary... but imperative! Do you understand me?"

Instinctively Lucy shrank away from him. Did she understand? Only too well!

"Is it because of my fortune? Is that why you are doing this?"

"Clever girl! Let's just say it was a considerable incentive!"

Nikolai had been right! How he would sneer at her for her gullibility! When Vasili had gone, silent tears rolled down her face. No use wishing now that she had never left Kamenoy Island.

"Nikolai come in!" The Tsar was seated in his study. He waved Nikolai into an adjacent chair.

"You've heard that Bonaparte wants me to meet him?" he continued. "I shall go, but I have given Barclay de Tolly and Bagration strict instructions: if the French set one foot on Russian soil, they are to fall back burning everything behind them. Bonaparte boasts that he will not rest until he has marched his Grande Armee into Moscow. I promise him that if he does he will have marched them into Hell. I have made Feodor Rostopchin Governor of Moscow, but he will take his orders from you." The Tsar smiled as he saw the other man's faint start. "After all, yours was the brain that conceived the plan in the first place! Besides I have more faith in your ability in an emergency than I do in Rostopchin's, able though he is."

"And if Bonaparte does get as far as Moscow?" Nikolai asked calmly.

"Then you will burn it to the ground. Bonaparte will never boast that he has possessed the birthplace of the Imperial family. And now, tell me how your grandfather goes on? He is to retire to Moscow next month, isn't he?"

Nikolai gave a bleak smile. "He does very well, but I mustn't delay you. I hear from my aunt that you are to attend a ball at the Rostov's on Kamenoy Island tonight. My cousin will be there."

"Your cousin?" The Tsar frowned. "I fear someone has tricked you Nikolai. It is true that I was invited to attend such a ball, but I had second thoughts. Certainly it is not a gathering I should wish to see a young, untried girl attending—not if she were my cousin." He emphasized the last few words slightly. Across the desk their eyes met, man to man.

"I am obliged to you, Sire. If you will excuse me?"

"Nikolai . . ."

He paused and looked back. "If your cousin has suffered any harm from this piece of mischief, you have my full permission to punish the perpetrators—as long as you do so discreetly."

Not a muscle moved in the mask-like face opposite him. When the door closed behind his visitor the Tsar sighed—poor Nikolai.

On quitting the Winter Palace Nikolai went first to his own home to question Tante Sophy about the arrangements for the evening. When she confirmed that Lucy had been reluctant to attend until she herself had persuaded her to, his frown lifted a little, although he did not divulge the information given to him by the Tsar.

Taking only Feodor as an ecort he set out for Kamenoy Island, his face so grimly closed against all questions that the manservant kept silent.

It was past two when they reached the island.

Although some couples still listened to the indefatigable gypsies, many had dispersed to seek privacy, and thus it was quite some time before Nikolai was able to discover the whereabouts of Lucy's supposed chaperone.

He had to question nearly half a dozen reluctant servants before he elicited the information that the Countess Molovskaya was with a certain Boris Pontemkin, a notorious rake who entertained his fellow officers with tales of his armorous intrigues. Nikolai's lip curled a little when he was eventually apprised where the Countess might be found.

Both she and her companion were furious at the interruption. Indeed the gentleman was on the point of buckling on his discarded sword until he saw who the intruder was. Although the Tsar had banned duels, Nikolai's reputation was such that even had they been permitted, Boris Pontemkin would have thought twice about challenging him.

Nikolai ignored his brother officer, concentrating all his attention upon the Countess. Lucy would have had a shock had she seen Anna at that moment, robbed of her lively prettiness by the hatred leaping into her eyes.

"It is too late now," she spat, shrugging off her lover's restraining arm. "Vasili will have made sure that she is forced to agree to their marriage!"

"Where has he taken her?" Nikolai asked tersely. "You might as well tell me, because I intend to find them even if I have to tear this place apart to do so!"

The Countess gave a mocking laugh. "Do so by all means. You will not find them here!"

Nikolai leaned forward and said slowly, emphasizing every word, "If I do not find them, all of St. Petersburg will learn what you are; and if one single word of tonight's affair becomes public knowledge, I shall see to it that you never dare to show your face in St. Petersburg again—and that goes for your friend as well! Now. Where is my cousin?"

Anna had paled as he spoke. She threw an appealing glance at her companion, but he was blind to her need.

"Vasili has taken her to the small island with the

111

summer house on it," she spat at him venomously. "Your silly little cousin will be glad enough to accept him as her husband once morning comes!"

He was gone almost before she had finished speaking. Feodor had to run to keep pace with him as he hurried down the steps to the jetty where the boats were moored. He had been often enough to parties here to pay no attention to what was going on about him, but his hands clenched as he thought of Lucy, and the trap the Orlovs had set for her.

"You will remain here," he commanded Feodor. When the manservant protested, he added curtly, "It is best that I go alone, because I promise you this: either Orlov or myself will return—but not both of us!"

Lucy had no way of telling how much time had passed. The sky still held a luminous pearlescence but she was in no mood to enjoy the beauties of nature. When she heard the first tentative footfall outside the door, she froze, knowing what her answer must be, no matter what it cost her. Generations of pride showed in the erect stance of her small body when the door swung open. She had her back to it, determined not to let Vasili see her betraying any sign of fear.

"If you have come for your answer, Count Orlov," she announced in a voice miraculously free of any tremor, "then I am bound to disappoint you. I shall never willingly give my consent to a match between us."

She turned as she spoke, determined to face whatever he had in store for her, but a small cry broke from her lips as she saw who was standing in the shadow of the door, of the summer house.

"Nikolai!" A relieved sob rose to her lips, refusing to be quenched.

"Are you all right?" The terse inquiry reminded her of the full horror of Vasili Orlov's threats.

"Yes," she replied unsteadily. "I'm very sorry to have put you to all this trouble."

Nikolai laughed harshly. "*This* trouble! Would to God that were all! You have caused me nothing *but* trouble from the moment we met. Now where is Orlov?"

"Right behind you," a voice sneered from the shadows. "So! I might have known you would interfere Kuragin, but you come too late. By tomorrow all the world will know that your cousin came to me willingly. How will your proud grandfather like that? He'll be glad enough to call me 'son-in-law' then!"

"I hate to contradict you, Orlov," Nikolai drawled softly, "but in this instance, you are too late. Lucy has already agreed to marry me. I have just this very evening sought the Tsar's agreement to our betrothal."

"Marry you!" Orlov's face contorted with rage. Vasili went for his sword, but Nikolai was ready for him. In that moment Lucy saw her erstwhile lover as he really was, without the mask he had worn for her benefit, and something deep inside her shrivelled and died. Vasili cared no more for her than he did for a starving peasant in the street. She was just so many hundreds of thousands of kopecks.

In a strained voice she begged Nikolai, "Do not fight with him. He is not worth it, and neither am I. I could not bear for you to lose your life in so worthless a cause. I should have listened to you in the first place."

In the second that Nikolai's attention was on Lucy, Vasili Orlov threw open the door and was gone before Nikolai could stop him. When he went to follow him, Lucy stood in his path.

"Please," she begged tiredly. "Let him go." She shivered suddenly, shaken with relief and reaction. Only one thought surfaced from the wreckage of her earlier trust in Vasili. She had to make her peace with Nikolai now, before her courage deserted her entirely. He had been right and she wrong, and she hoped she was not mean-spirited enough to refuse to admit as much.

"It was good of you to say we were to be married," she began formally. "I thank you for it, especially . . ."

Nikolai wasn't listening. He swore suddenly, glancing out of the window. "Damn! Orlov has cast my boat adrift. I should have thought . . . ."

Lucy joined him, looking over his shoulder. Sure

enough a small boat was bobbing merrily up and down in the current carrying it away from the island.

"Does it really matter?" she asked dispiritedly. "I confess, though, that I would rather not spend the night here."

"Especially not with me, I take it."

When Lucy gave him a puzzled look, he elucidated harshly. "Have you forgotton already that you 'hate' me cousin? And why?"

Lucy moved hurriedly away from him. She would not break down, not now. Not until she was safe in her own room and could give vent to her shocked horror in privacy.

"Be that as it may," Nikolai continued. "There is one thing I must make plain here and now. I have told Orlov we are betrothed. That betrothal must stand. Do you understand me, Lucy?"

Lucy looked up at him piteously. "You cannot mean that," she whispered. "We cannot be betrothed."

"We *must* be," Nikolai retorted with iron determination. "Surely you cannot suppose society will look any more kindly on your spending the night here with me than had you been with Orlov. I assure you they will not!"

Lucy shivered, her eyes huge in her small face. "But they will not know," she protested. "There is no need . . ."

"You may be sure Orlov will spread the tale, from spite if nothing else," Nikolai replied flatly. "However, what we are talking about is merely a fictional betrothal— nothing more. Fortunately we shall be able to keep tonight's business from grandpère. You will be leaving St. Petersburg with him soon. Once you are gone we shall put it about that we did not suit, and that will be an end to the matter."

He spoke so matter-of-factly that Lucy could find no reason to object. As she stared out of the window, watching the small boat floating ever further away, Nikolai removed his coat and handed it to her.

"Here, take this," he instructed. "Your skirts are all damp, and you will take a chill if you do not have a care. We could be here some time before we are rescued."

He didn't tell her what he had said to Feodor or what conclusions his servants would come to when Vasili Orlov stepped ashore. A muscle beat under his skin, and the scar on his face seemed more noticeable than before.

Lucy hung her head. "I'm sorry I disobeyed you, Nikolai."

The words were so low that her companion had to strain to catch them. Her silly temper had brought them to this pass. It was only by the merest chance that neither Vasili nor Nikolai was lying dead at her feet at this very moment, and all through her own wretched defiance.

"The blame is as much mine as yours, if we are to apportion it fairly," Nikolai responded tiredly. "I should have realized that a girl of spirit would take umbrage at being told where to make her friends, but I know Orlov of old." He seemed about to add something and then stopped frowning darkly. "You must not let this mock betrothal worry you. By this time next year it will all be forgotten. Far easier to overcome a broken betrothal than a broken reputation, as you will soon discover."

For some foolish, feminine reason, these words brought remorseful tears stingingly to Lucy's eyes. It was too much to hope that Nikolai had not noticed this silly weakness. His eyebrows rose. "You cry? For Orlov? Can you not see what he is, even now?"

He sounded so angry that Lucy stepped back.

"Dear God," he muttered "You look at *me* with fear in your eyes, and yet for Orlov, who would ruin you to secure your fortune, you . . ."

She wanted to tell him that it was not as he imagined, but shyness held her tongue captive, and she could only stare uncomprehendingly at him as his face darkened in sudden inexplicable anger. His hands reached out, grasping her arms, his eyes no longer cold, but hotly angry.

"So far you have shown me anger, contempt, and now fear, little cousin. Now it is my turn to give rein to *my* feelings!"

There was anger in the pressure of his mouth on hers. A punishment Lucy decided bleakly, as his arms crushed her against his chest. But there was something

115

else there as well! Something unbearably sweet that seemed to sap her strength, and turn her blood into fiery passion, melting her resistance, and unveiling a thousand emotions she had never before guessed existed. Almost instinctively her body relaxed, sensing what her mind had not yet comprehended. When Nikolai wrenched his mouth away, the shock was as great as being plunged into the icy wastes of the Neva. Only the muscle pulsing betrayingly in his jaw hinted at the passions he was holding in control, but Lucy was too unversed in the ways of men to know the significance of his clenched hands and taut face.

"There! now you know that I am no more to be trusted than Orlov, and no doubt you will bear it in mind for the future! With any luck, Feodor should be here before too long. You need not fear that you will have to spend another night in my company!"

"And . . . and our betrothal?" Lucy asked hesitantly.

"That can wait upon events. Should Orlov choose to make tonight's affair public, we shall have no other choice, but until he makes a move we shall say nothing. Believe me the thought of entering such a contract is as abhorrent to me as it is to you!"

Eight

Those words continued to ring in Lucy's ears in the days after their return from the island. Indeed, she found herself brooding unhappily over them when her attention should have been elsewhere, such as on the book she was reading to grandpère or on the item of gossip Tante Sophy was so busy relating to her.

It was over a week since the nightmare events that had brought her so near to the edge of ruin. She had not seen Nikolai at all since he had deposited her outside the Kuragin Palace.

Had Vasili carried out his threats to ruin her reputation, she wondered worriedly? Lucy had no way of knowing. She shivered a little despite the warmth of the library fire. The date for their departure to Moscow had been brought forward to the end of the week, and she suspected Nikolai had had a hand in its alteration. As he had said, without their presence to feed the gossip, it would soon die down. Her fingers strayed to her lips—lips that still seemed to feel the vivid imprint of his. Why did he not come? He must know how anxious she was.

Tante Sophy bustled in, frowning over Lucy's abstracted air. Anyone would think the child had fallen in love, she thought despairingly, for she bore all the signs of a girl with her mind on "other things."

"Nikolai has just arrived," she informed Lucy. "He is with your grandfather."

Lucy's heart lurched against her ribs. "Did he . . . did he ask for me?"

"I don't think so. Ought he to have done?"

As far as the events on the island were concerned, Tante Sophy knew only what Nikolai had chosen to tell her, which was very little, but Lucy's high color stirred her curiosity. Fortunately, before she could give voice to it, the door opened and Nikolai walked in.

"May I have a moment with Lucy, Tante Sophy?" he requested. "In private!"

The older woman's eyes rounded a little speculatively, but she made no comment, whisking herself out of the room before Lucy could so much as open her mouth to protest.

It is all over town that we were alone together, unchaperoned, on the island," Nikolai informed her without preamble, once they were alone. "That is Orlov's revenge for your refusal, of course. I'm afraid I have had no alternative but to refute the gossip by announcing our betrothal. However, there is a complication I had not considered. Grandpère had a visit from General Romansky this morning."

Lucy waited, while the suspense grew. Nikolai was looking extremely grave.

"I'm afraid the General had heard about our 'betrothal' and congratulated grandpère."

"Oh no!"

"Oh yes! I have just had to undergo a very uncomfortable thirty minutes with grandpère trying to explain why *he* was not the first to know of our plans. I think I've managed to calm him. When he's stronger, of course, we will be able to tell him the truth, but for now it is perhaps wiser to allow him his dreams . . ."

Lucy swallowed painfully. "You mean he *approves* of our betrothal?"

" Can you doubt it? His joy knows no bounds. However," Nikolai continued in neutral accents, "matters are not as grave as they might be. I have persuaded him that for the time being the announcement will not be made public. I have reminded him that the proximity of war

118

precludes me from spending a great deal of time with you, and I have suggested that things be left on an informal basis until your return to St. Petersburg in the autumn. As far as the gossips are concerned, the mere fact that there is an 'understanding' between us will draw the venom from their sting, and you need fear no reprisals in that direction. I suggest that the best thing we can do is to let matters take care of themselves. By the time winter comes, grandpère should be strong enough to stand the truth; and let me assure you here and now, that I have no designs upon either your person or your fortune."

"I didn't think you did have!" Lucy retorted, stung.

He smiled sardonically. "No? I thought perhaps our last exchange might have placed ideas in your head which have no business to be there."

"I did not think because you kissed me, you wanted me for your wife, if that's what you mean!"

"Very wise of you," came the dry retort.

It was shortly after that, that Nikolai left, but not before Tante Sophy had been invited to share their "news." Happily, her own enthusiasm and delight was such that she had no time to spare to notice the less than lover-like behavior of the newly affianced pair. Only the fact that they were shortly to leave St. Petersburg prevented her from making lavish plans for a summer wedding—much to Lucy's relief.

Nikolai was not allowed to leave until Tante Sophy had extracted from him a promise to visit them should he chance to get leave during the coming months. For, as Tante Sophy put it to Lucy once they were alone; "You may be sure the Tsar will be disposed to look favorably upon the match; and if it wasn't for this horrid war, which everyone says we may expect, I am sure he would be happy to grant Nikolai leave of absence."

Lucy made a non-committal response. It was hard enough to preserve an outward appearance of pleasure in her betrothal, without having the constant and intimidating presence of her "betrothed" to contend with as well. To think that she had actually welcomed the General, too! Fair-mindedly she was forced to admit that she and Nikolai had been caught in their own trap. She glanced down at her hand. A huge sapphire surrounded by diamonds glittered there. Nikolai had placed it on her finger, in grandpère's presence, not an hour before.

Tante Sophy, who had been inspecting the ring, frowned suddenly. "I cannot understand it. Never have I seen that ring before, and I am familiar with every piece of the Kuragin jewelry. My dearest sister showed me the entire collection when she married Ivan Ivanovitch. But that ring . . ."

"Perhaps it comes from Nikolai's mama's family," Lucy suggested.

"Perhaps!" Tante Sophy gave her a shrewd look. "However, personally I favor another explanation. Nikolai had it made especially for you, you silly goose. It is so exactly the same color as your eyes."

"Oh surely not!" In her agitation Lucy twisted the ring around her finger.

Tante Sophy laughed. "But of course! What could be more flattering? Or more romantic? It is all just as I hoped. The moment I set eyes on you, I knew you would be just right for Nikolai!"

There was a good deal more in the same vein, which left Lucy feeling both uncomfortable and unhappy. And there was still more to be endured.

If Tante Sophy's enthusiasm had not shown her the folly of entering into such a charade—no matter how well meant—grandpère's must surely have done.

Although nowhere near as verbose as his sister-in-law, grandpère nevertheless was equally delighted with the betrothal. So much so that the tentative idea that she might confess the whole to him, now, before any further damage was done, died almost at birth. In his present weakened condition, such a disclosure would surely prove highly prejudicial to his full recovery.

Fortunately, with the preparations for their departure to Moscow there was no time for Lucy to dwell too deeply upon the evils of her situation.

A huge carriage, such as she had never dreamed

existed, was dragged out of the stables and prepared for the journey. Drawn by a team of horses, it possessed not only a bedroom, but also a completely separate sitting room, all fitted out so neatly and so compactly that Lucy could only marvel at the workmanship which had gone into it.

"It is modelled on the carriages made for the Empress Catherine," Tante Sophy told her. "And very necessary too, when one is travelling long distances. Your grandfather will travel in one of the carriages with a manservant to look after him, and you and I will travel in another."

The long cavalcade eventually set forth from St. Petersburg some days later. Nikolai had not come to see them off, much to Lucy's private relief, although she did feel rather a fraud when Tante Sophy commiserated with her, and praised her for her understanding.

"Lucy knows Nikolai would be with her if he could," Grandpère said, patting her hand. "But in the present state of emergency . . . ."

The news of Napoleon's invasion had broken only the day before. All St. Petersburg was agog with it. The French had crossed the Neimen, and the Tsar had gone to join his troops, taking his personal regiment with him.

The French were advancing on Smolensk, the ancient capital of Holy Russia, and the Russian troops were falling back under their advance.

Lucy knew next to nothing of warfare, but it seemed a poor thing to be doing.

"Tactics," Grandpère had announced in a gruff voice that told Lucy he too found the Tsar's decision less than valorous.

Even so, despite the thunder clouds of war looming on the horizon, nothing occured to disrupt their journey to Moscow, and Lucy had her first taste of the vastness of the Russian plain. Peasants in tiny villages stopped to stare after them. Ragged children ran alongside the carriages. Lucy kept a bag of small coins handy to throw to them, although Tante Sophy did not totally approve.

"You must not encourge them to beg," she reproved

in one village where the children seemed particularly ill-cared for. "On our own estates, no child needs to go hungry or to dress in rags."

Lucy was relieved to hear it. She was looking forward to seeing the huge estate that would one day be Nikolai's. She knew grandpère owned other estates spread over the country, but this particular one had always been the family home.

They reached Moscow on the third day. It was evening when they paused by the Hill of Sparrows to stare across the river at the old walled Kremlin. The late afternoon sun dyed the gilded towers of St. Basil's red gold. Lucy caught her breath in amazement: never had she anticipated anything so very Eastern in concept; so very different from the elegant grandeur of St Petersburg.

"The birthplace of Russia," Grandpère murmured emotionally. "Every Tsar is crowned within the Kremlin. It is the most Holy; the most cherished of all our cities. When I am feeling a little better, you shall see it properly. I hope you will come to love it as we all do."

The Kuragin Estate was some way out of Moscow, set among rolling hills, an old, mellowed house exuding an air of homely contentment. Lucy fell in love with it at first sight. Generations of Kuragins had added to and extended the original building, until it resembled a cluster of mismatched domed buildings, tinted crimson in the last rays of the sun.

Willing hands helped ease travel-weary bodies from the carriages, and Lucy noticed how gentle and caring the serfs were with her grandfather. Plainly this was no callous landlord riding roughshod over his people but more a beloved patriarch.

She was given the rooms which had once been her mama's with a view over the plain toward Moscow. On a clear day it was sometimes possible to see the glitter of the sun reflected on the towers of St. Basil's, Tante Sophy informed her as she instructed a maid to help her unpack.

"For myself, I am not over-fond of the country," she

added. "You will find there is little to do but pay calls on one's neighbors and supervise the household, but Ivan Ivanovitch prefers Moscow to St. Petersburg."

In the days that followed Lucy learned to understand why: one of the serfs, at grandpère's command, took her to the stables and helped her choose a mount. She had always enjoyed riding and now, with the serf as her constant companion and guide, she set out to explore her new environment.

There was so much to see and do that time flew by. They heard that Napoleon was marching on Smolensk and that, as yet, the Russian Army had made no stand against him. There were also the calls Tante Sophy had mentioned to her. Away from St. Petersburg, Lucy had removed her engagement ring. "For safety's sake," she had informed her shocked aunt. But if she had hoped by so doing to prevent news of her betrothal from spreading, she was doomed to disappointment. Indeed Tante Sophy seemed to derive the greatest enjoyment from informing her visitors of her "happy" news.

It was a hot summer, and Lucy took to riding in the early morning while the dew was still on the ground, curling upward in faint tendrils, as the sun dispersed it.

One of her favorite rides was through a small birch glade which contained a pool, set in its depths like a clear, green emerald, within a tracery of silver.

One morning, about a month after her arrival in Moscow, she reached the pool and dismounted to discover that she was not alone. A young girl was seated beside the pool, engrossed in a volume she was studying, a baby in a rush basket at her side.

Wondering if the girl came from the village on the Kuragin Estate, Lucy started to talk to her, but she was too frightened to make any response. At Lucy's approach she had cast down her book, and when Lucy tried a few words of her newly learned Russian, the girl ignored her, hurriedly gathering up her baby.

Lucy caught her arm. "It's all right really. There's no need to go just because I'm here. Your baby is lovely. What is his name?"

The reference to her child brought a proud smile to the young mother's face.

"He is named Alexander," she informed Lucy shyly in hesitant French.

Where had she learned to speak that language, Lucy wondered, looking at her rough homespun gown and coarse linen apron. Her clothes were those of a peasant girl, but her manner was that of an upper servant of some description. Lucy knew that many of the St. Petersburg servants spoke some French, but so far, on the estate, she had had to rely on her sketchy Russian to make herself understood. She grew curious about the girl and wanted to question her further, but when she tried, a strange, shuttered expression came down over the girl's face. Picking up her baby, she disengaged herself from Lucy's grasp and hurried off into the wood. Puzzled, Lucy stared after her, wondering what had made her act in such a very odd manner.

She mentioned the matter at the dinner table. Tante Sophy looked surprised.

"A serving girl who reads? You must be mistaken, child."

"Someone from the village then?" Lucy persisted.

"Even less likely," Grandpère commented. "We have enough trouble getting the boys to attend school. The time will come when every serf will learn to read and write, but that time is not yet, Lucy."

The incident continued to haunt her. There had been something so very timorous in the girl's eyes, almost as though she had expected Lucy to chastise her for something. She had been a pretty girl too, Lucy recalled, with soft, brown eyes and a slender body. She questioned several of the household serfs, but all of them denied any knowledge of such a person, until Lucy began to think she had dreamed the meeting. Then one afternoon when she was riding through a small clearing in the forest, she thought she glimpsed her again. Calling to her groom she bade him dismount and go after her. Ten minutes later he returned, hot and perspiring.

"She has disappeared, Barina," he reported.

Really, Lucy thought in exasperation, it was almost as though there were some sort of conspiracy to prevent her from talking to the girl again. But why? She was determined to get to the bottom of the mystery. On the way back she questioned her groom. At first reluctant to answer, he gave way when she threatened to comb the woods herself, inch by inch, if necessary, in order to find the girl.

"She lives alone just outside the village."

"Alone?" Lucy queried. "Has she no family . . . no husband?"

"The girl is a wanton," the groom replied gruffly. "Last winter she went to St. Petersburg. When she returned she had a child but no husband. She has brought shame upon her village. Her presence there is only tolerated because Prince Nikolai commands it . . ."

"Prince Nikolai!?" Lucy interrupted sharply.

All at once everything fell into place. Could the girl be the same one Vasili had accused Nikolai of seducing? It seemed all too likely. There could be no other reason for him to take such a personal interest in her. Which meant that the child . . . . Grimly Lucy dug her heels into her mount's sides. Many men of Nikolai's rank fathered such children, she knew, but to desert the mother and allow the child to be brought up in shame and disgrace. . . .

Well, if no one else intended to remonstrate with her cousin for his callousness, she certainly did! What would grandpère say if he knew the truth about his precious grandson? But Lucy knew that she could never be the one to tell him.

It was only later, as they approached the house, that she realized that the girl might possibly still care deeply for Nikolai, and resent her own presence, thinking she had supplanted her in his affections, for all the estate workers knew of their "betrothal." She must seek out the girl and talk to her, Lucy decided as she dismounted in the stable yard. It was wrong that she should be made to

125

suffer, while Nikolai escaped from the liaison unscathed.

Unfortunately, this was easier said than done. It was several days before Lucy had enough time to herself to search for her quarry.

Quite by chance her route to the village took her past the pool where she had surprised the girl before, and to her delight, Lucy saw that she was there again.

Dismissing her groom, she dismounted and approached. As she had half expected, the moment she saw her the girl leapt to her feet, ready to flee.

"Don't go!" Lucy commanded. "I want to talk to you. I know all about what happened in St. Petersburg," she continued, "and I am very sorry for it. It is a pity that your baby will not grow up to be more proud of his father, but the blame for that does not lie with you. I shall see to it that my cousin is made aware of his responsibilities and forced to do the right thing by his child . . ."

The girl who had been listening to her in silence up until this point, stared at her in dismay.

"The Barina does not think . . . you cannot imagine . . . that Prince Nikolai is the father of my child," she stammered.

"Your wish to defend him does you credit, but I have already been informed of my cousin's infamous behavior," Lucy told her.

To her surprise the girl's eyes flashed in anger. "Then the Barina has been *misinformed,* for it is not Prince Nikolai who is the father of my child, but another, who cravenly seeks to hide his sin by laying it at the door of someone else."

Now it was Lucy's turn to stare. There was no doubt that the girl was telling the truth. Loyal indignation showed in every word she spoke.

When Lucy remained silent she added proudly, "I wish I might claim the Prince as my child's father. He alone protected me in my shame, bringing me home and providing me with somewhere to live."

If Nikolai was not the father of the girl's child, then who was? It was a question Lucy had to ask.

At first the girl was reluctant to tell her, but her

eagerness to clear Nikolai's name at length overcame her diffidence.

"It was Count Orlov who fathered my child," she admitted at last. "He came often to the Kuragin Palace with his sister, who was betrothed to the Prince, and he would seek me out." Her eyes misted over with tears. "Perhaps I was foolish, but I believed him when he said he loved me . . . I did not think . . . ."

Lucy's tender heart was touched with compassionate pity, followed instantly by contemptuous anger toward the man she had once admired. How clever Vasili had been, playing on her susceptibilities, poisoning her mind against Nikolai, when in fact, *he* had been the guilty party.

And what about Anna? She had deliberately deceived her, Lucy realized. Had her reasons for the breaking of her betrothal to Nikolai been equally fictitious?

It was a very thoughtful young lady who rode back toward the house.

At the point where the track joined the main road to Moscow, Lucy heard hoofbeats behind her. Thinking it was her groom, she reined in to wait. As the rider drew nearer she recognized the features of Vasili Orlov, and anger welled up inside her.

Vasili approached with a smile, not realizing that Lucy had discovered the extent of his perfidy. As he drew level with her, he caught at her reins.

"Today must be my lucky day. When your groom told me that you were some way down this road, I thought I might have to search for an hour or more to find you."

Lucy was amazed at his bold assumption that they were still the best of friends. Had he forgotton so quickly the circumstances of their parting?

If so, she certainly had not; and if it weren't for the fact that she intended to tell him exactly what she thought of him, she would have ridden off without bothering to acknowledge him. She had no choice in the matter, however because he was now grasping her reins quite tightly.

"Please release me, Vasili," she demanded. "I cannot think what you are doing here. You and I can have nothing to say to each other. And before you do say anything, I must tell you that I now know the full story of your deceit."

If she had expected him to display remorse, she was sadly disappointed. He merely shrugged dismissively, drawing her horse closer to his own.

"That was Anna's idea. I swear I never thought we should deceive you so easily, but you were bound to learn the truth sooner or later. Who told you, Kuragin?"

Lucy was appalled at his lack of concern.

"Have you no shame? No pity for the girl you so cruelly wronged; no care for her child—your child!"

Indifference had given way to anger as she spoke and now he said in a hard voice, "What is done is done. The girl has no claims on me, and as for the child, that might be anybody's!"

"You truly are beneath contempt," Lucy said, temper scarcely under control. "If you are not gone from these lands within the hour I shall command our people to use force to remove you . . ."

To her amazement Vasili only laughed "I shall be gone all right," he jeered, "and you will be gone with me. 'Tis better this way, for I need not bother to adopt any loverlike pose. Thanks to you and your interfering cousin, my creditors will wait no longer. My sister writes that I must not show my face in St. Petersburg, and so I have deserted from my regiment—a regiment I can no longer afford, and the only way out of my present predicament is for me to find myself a rich bride—you!"

Lucy wrenched her horse's head around, but it was too late. Vasili, stronger than her by far, gripped her arm, holding it tightly as he fastened her reins to his own.

"Oh no you don't," he said softly. "I have ventured too much to lose you now!"

"You forget that I am betrothed to Nikolai!" Lucy protested, but he silenced her with a cold sneer.

"Indeed you are, but, between us, Anna and I will make sure St. Petersburg knows you preferred me! The fact that I am taking you from Kuragin merely adds salt to the meat my dear. Now, are you going to be sensible, or do I have to prove how determined I am by tying you to your mount? I want to be gone from here before that groom of yours raises the alarm—not that a sick old man and an empty-headed female will be able to prevent me from taking you."

Lucy realized that it could be several hours before anyone discovered she was missing, thanks to her own folly in dismissing her groom. But she tried to take comfort from the thought that once they did, they would surely understand that the man who had inquired of her from the groom must be her abductor. Grandpère, at least, would never believe she had gone willingly with Vasili!

"Hurry!" Vasili snarled at her side. "Bonaparte has captured Smolensk. You could see it burning for miles. Soon the French will be in Moscow. You should be thanking me, my dear. After all, think what I have saved you from. They say the French are in no mood to remember the niceties of life. Apparently, they are near to starving, thanks to our noble Tsar's decision to raze the crops and drive off all the cattle.

Not once during that appalling journey to Moscow did Lucy deign to speak to her captor. Not even to ask him why he was taking her to a city which he himself had said would shortly be invaded by the French.

However, she knew soon enough.

"Before this night is over, we shall be married," Vasili told her. "Anna's idea—her way of getting her own back, I doubt not. Your lofty cousin is choosy when it comes to his wife it appears, and Anna had been foolish enough to engage in a . . . well let us call it a light diversion . . . while he was out of St. Petersburg. Unfortunately, someone told him about it, and our cold, proud Prince let it be known that unless she broke off the betrothal he would have no option but to do so for her. You may forget any illusions you are cherishing that he will seek to recover you. Once you become my wife, you become my property, and a very rich and rewarding property, I am sure you will prove, too."

Lucy felt sick with fear and anger.

"Can you blame him?" Lucy retorted bitterly.

Vasili's only response was to gather her reins more tightly and dig his spurs into his horse's side. The animal was weary and travel-stained, but he seemed to care nothing for its discomfort. How the scales had fallen from her eyes, Lucy thought wearily.

By tomorrow morning she would be this man's wife. She had never wanted anything less in all her life, not even her betrothal to Nikolai. How she had misjudged her cousin. Vasili was right about one thing, however, Nikolai would never forgive her for giving Vasili the opportunity to humiliate him. What agonies of mind she would have suffered had theirs been a real betrothal, and had she been condemned to marry the most bitter enemy of the man she loved. She choked back a frightened sob. Almost she could wish that the French had reached Moscow; but as they rode into the city, there was no one to challenge their entry, no one to make a protest, no one to save her from the unpleasant fate shortly to be hers!

Vasili took her to a house nestling within the Kremlin Wall, constructed of timber and plasterwork, and obviously very old. A servant opened the door to his imperative knock, her fear at the sight of her master such that even if Lucy had previously cherished no doubts about her companion, she must surely have done so then.

She was escorted to a room, stale and musty with disuse, heavy curtains shadowing the narrow windows, and no fire in the grate. The servant brought them rye bread and cheese, and then left.

"She has gone to summon a Priest," Vasili informed Lucy. "Prepare yourself, my dear, for we shall be wed before the night is out. How do you like the place I have chosen for your honeymoon?"

Her expression gave her away. Wide, frightened eyes resting briefly on his mocking face before they flew to the window, like a bird seeking escape.

Vasili seated himself on one of the chairs. He was wearing his uniform, mud-stained and filthy from his flight from Smolensk. He shrugged off his great coat letting it fall to the floor.

A fine bridal pair they would make, Lucy thought hysterically, with the bride in a riding dress and the groom in a uniform that looked as though it had not been changed in days.

In that assumption she was quite correct. The Tsar's army had been engaged in several skirmishes as they fell back before the French, and Vasili had made good use of one of them to make his escape. Once the news of Lucy's betrothal to Nikolai had broken in St. Petersburg, his creditors had come down on him like a pack of wolves on a wounded hind. He had conceived the idea of marrying Lucy by force after Anna had told him that she had retired to the Kuragin Estate. That way he could kill two birds with one stone—injure Nikolai and get himself a rich wife. He glanced across at Lucy. Unaware of his scrutiny she sat in an upright chair, staring out of the window.

"There is no Kuragin to rescue you this time," he mocked. "He is with the Tsar still, at Smolensk. By the time he hears what has happened you could be carrying his first nephew."

He gave a cruel laugh when Lucy turned horror-struck eyes toward him, a denial trembling on her lips.

"You hadn't thought of that? I had. With a great deal of pleasure." His lips twisted in a sardonic smile. I'm sure the old Prince will look far more favorably on me when he knows I have fathered his first great-grandchild."

"As you fathered that poor serf's?" Lucy burst out, too incensed to question the wisdom of provoking her captor.

His response was to grip her arm with cruelly hurtful fingers, though her eyes defiantly told him of her contempt.

"You will soon sing a different song, my pretty," he sneered unkindly.

The lengthening shadows lent the shabby room a subtly sinister air. Faint noises outside the room impinged upon the silence. The sound of a door opening and then closing. Voices, which grew louder as footsteps approached the room.

"This will be the priest," Vasili announced triumphantly, going to the door.

Lucy shrank back, dreading the arrival of the man who was to tie her to Vasili. In the shadowy darkness all she could see was a tall figure wrapped in a dark cloak.

Her abductor laughed softly, watching with malice-filled eyes. "Make up your mind to accept it, my dear, there is no escape for you."

"Nor any for you, Orlov," the "priest" promised dangerously, removing his cloak and revealing to Lucy's startled eyes the person of her cousin.

For several seconds there was a throbbing silence and then Lucy started forward, "Nikolai . . ."

He motioned her back with a wave of his hand, and in the confusion which followed, Lucy could be sure of nothing, save that somehow Nikolai had found her, and was standing between her and Vasili. The old serving woman wrung her hands under the storm of abuse Vasili unleashed upon her when she protested that she had not been able to prevent Nikolai from entering.

"Fool," he raged through clenched teeth, "imbecile . . ." He aimed a blow at her unprotected head, only to be intercepted by Nikolai, one hand on Vasili's arm, the other on his own sword hilt.

"So that's to be the way of it, is it?" Vasili sneered.

"I shall enjoy killing you, Prince. I have staked too much to risk losing now."

"You will leave us, Lucy," Nikolai commanded without taking his eyes off Vasili's face.

She wanted to protest, but he was already removing his dress sword from its scabbard. The fading light flickered briefly on the honed metal, and the significance of his carefully measured actions suddenly struck her. He was going to challenge Vasili to a duel! Her eyes went instinctively to the livid scar on his face.

"Nikolai, no! Do not!" she begged.

She might as well not have spoken. The old woman

was holding the door open. Nikolai removed his shoes without another look in her direction.

"I am giving you a chance you do not deserve, Orlov," she heard Nikolai say emotionlessly as the servant drew Lucy out through the door. "The chance to die like a gentleman and not like the vermin that you are!"

Nine

The sound of the key turning in the lock was unnaturally loud in the taut silence of the room. Nikolai pocketed it and faced his adversary.

"What I ought to do is take my whip to your back, but this will be more final."

"You haven't killed me yet," Vasili sneered. "The last time we fought I left you with that scar."

"The last time we fought I was foolish enough to lay down my sword when I thought you were injured. That was my first mistake. The second was not realizing that you would attack me while I was unarmed. My third was that I let you live. This time there will be no mistakes."

The rapiers clashed together, and then disengaged, without the preliminary niceties of the en garde position. Vasili used the advantage he had gained from attacking, to aim his blade at his opponent's heart, but Nikolai was ready for him, shrugging easily aside. The blade rang together again, both men falling silent as they each struggled for supremacy.

Nikolai's was the greater strength and skill, but he was hampered by his growing exhaustion. Vasili was a man fighting for his life, and the fading daylight flickering on the white scar across the other's cheek warned him that the price for failure would not be abated.

"What brought you here with such untimely haste?" He could see that Nikolai was tiring and hoped to prolong their duel long enough to catch him off guard. "Don't tell me the great Nikolai Kuragin was running from the burning fires of Smolensk like a common soldier after his first taste of war?" he mocked.

Nikolai's mouth tightened but he didn't respond to the thrust. "The Tsar gave me command of a troop he has sent to prepare the defense of Moscow. It was only by the merest chance that we learned that you were travelling in this direction. Someone mentioned having seen a soldier wearing a Hussar's uniform riding through one of the villages. I was curious about the business which took that 'soldier' so far from the battle. In fact, I would have caught up with you earlier had my horse not cast a shoe. As it was I decided to go home, since I was so very close." His voice was grim. "As luck would have it I met my cousin's groom just as he was on his way to raise the alarm."

"Fortune favors you—and me, for it gives me the opportunity to bring our . . . association, to a fitting end."

As he spoke, Vasili lunged forward hard. Nikolai parried instantly, his reflexes marginally slower than usual so that instead of missing him completely the blade glanced along his arm, slicing through the thin fabric of his shirt and leaving a deep scratch in his flesh. Blood welled into the wound, falling in bright scarlet drops onto the dusty floor.

"Not so proud now, my fine friend," Vasili sneered. "You are nearing the end of your strength, why not admit it?"

"Why don't you prove it?" Nikolai retorted through gritted teeth.

Unlike Vasili he had not had time to rest on the journey from Smolensk. The wound in his arm ached, but he ignored it, summoning the last reserves of his strength.

Concentrating all his flagging energy on his opponent, he started to drive Vasili backward into a corner, his eyes never leaving the other man's face. There was hard determination in that green gaze, and something else that made Vasili Orlov falter and glance nervously over his shoulder, as though he feared something might lurk in the shadows behind him.

Nikolai's blade broke through Vasili's guard, disengaging to slide up underneath his rapier and rest for a second at the base of his throat.

"I could kill you now, Orlov, but I won't. I want you to share a little of the agony you have inflicted on others, before you die," he said softly.

The blade pricked the sweat-beaded skin and was removed, leaving Vasili to summon what was left of his courage and try to protect himself from what he was slowly becoming convinced was no mere human swordsman, but the devil incarnate, such incredible skill and speed did the other possess.

"Even if you kill me, you cannot hope to survive," he panted, when he had been forced to give way, yet again. "Smolensk is taken. The Russian Army will be forced to stand and fight against the French, and when they do, they will be defeated. How long, do you suppose, a member of the Tsar's Personal Guard will live once Bonaparte controls Moscow?"

"Moscow will never be taken," Nikolai told him curtly lunging forward.

Exhaustion slowing his reactions, Vasili parried just in time. "You think not?" He raised a hand to dash the sweat from his eyes. "Who is going to protect it? The Tsar who ran away from Austerlitz in tears?"

He never saw the blade; never felt the impact of it piercing his breast bone; only a terrible, implacable pain and a wave of dark red mist that covered everything but the grim face of his opponent.

Outside Lucy crouched by the door, ignoring the old woman's pleas to accompany her to another room. Through the thick wood she heard the muted sounds of the duel taking place within. The soft footfalls of the two men. The hissing clash of steel on steel. The occasional muttered comment, too low for her to catch, and then a silence which was unnervingly complete.

She heard footsteps and closed her eyes, clenching her hands.

The door opened and her eyes flew open. A man

came toward her, his body rigid with exhaustion, his sweat-streaked hair, ruffled and untidy.

"Nikolai!" she whispered his name through a throat, aching with suppressed tears.

"How did you know what had happened? Where I was?" she asked weakly, closing her eyes against the sight of the still figure lying on the floor behind him. "And what are you doing in Moscow?"

He shrugged wearily, flexing his shoulders. "I am in Moscow on the Tsar's orders. As to the rest . . . . we had had news of a Hussar riding ahead of us from the villages we rode through on our way to Moscow, but it wasn't until your groom came up to the house to see if you had returned that I began to suspect the truth. When he described the man who had spoken to him I knew it had to be Orlov, until then I had thought the Hussar merely another deserter."

"And this house?" Lucy asked bemused by the quirk of fate that had decreed that Nikolai should leave Smolensk virtually at the same time as Vasili. Only Nikolai had been acting on the orders of the Tsar, and Vasili a deserter, who had made no bones about the plans he had for her. Her head drooped.

"Anna stayed here when she was in Moscow. I used to visit her here," he explained briefly. "I could only guess that Orlov would bring you here." His mouth compressed. "Your groom should be whipped for letting you ride unattended. When I think of what could have occurred had I not decided to make use of a few spare hours by riding out to the estate . . . ."

"You must not blame the groom," Lucy said in a low voice. "The fault was mine. I dismissed him. Tante Sophy must . . . ."

"I asked her to tell grandpère that you had taken to your bed with a sick headache, and reassured her as best I could. Your groom has been warned to say nothing of Orlov. I shall escort you back to the estate." His voice was cold, the voice of an irate parent to an erring child, Lucy thought wearily. Nikolai was watching her. He saw the shadow lying under her eyes in mauve pools and frowned. "Neither of us is in any fit state to make the journey tonight."

"You cannot be suggesting that we stay *here*," Lucy protested. A shudder trembled through her. She could not forget what had so nearly happened in this house. Were they to remain here she was sure she would not get so much as a wink of sleep. And then there was Vasili. Hate him though she now did, he had paid for his sins with his life, and she could not remain in the same house as his mortal remains.

As though he knew what was going through her mind Nikolai pushed her out of the room, closing the door, his expression suggesting that he was having difficulty keeping his temper under control.

"I haven't slept properly in three nights, Lucy, and neither have my men. We have sustained a major defeat. The French have taken Smolensk. The Tsar has sent me to Moscow to . . . to make certain arrangements to prevent it from falling into French hands. Time is short, and I have much to do. I have a house just inside the Kremlin Walls. You will be quite safe there, and tomorrow I shall escort you back to Tante Sophy."

He spoke quite dispassionately, but Lucy had the distinct impression that she was a complication he could well do without.

"I'm sorry," she whispered, unsure exactly what she was apologizing for, for surely she could not be blamed for Vasili Orlov's sudden appearance nor his intended abducton of her? She knew she ought to apologize to Nikolai for castigating him so heedlessly for Vasili's sins, but for some reason she felt acutely embarrassed and tongue-tied. She could feel the warm color seeping into her skin as Nikolai looked at her, and she looked away hurriedly, confused by her own emotions.

This was not the way to behave, she scolded herself. Taking a deep breath she faced her cousin.

"Nikolai, I owe you an apology. I should never have paid any heed to either of the Orlovs. I know now just how much they wronged you."

To her relief Nikolai seemed prepared to accept her

apology. "Orlov had his reasons for acting as he did. There had been emnity between us for many years. No doubt he saw marriage to you as a means of securing not only a large fortune but also of paying me back."

"Yes, he did," Lucy agreed. "He told me so. What a fool I was. Do you know, I actually believed he cared about me?"

Despite her care, her voice wobbled traitorously. Nikolai's hand rested on her arm for a second and was then withdrawn. All at once Lucy had a longing to be taken in his arms and to lay her head against his shoulder. Because I miss papa, she told herself, and Nikolai is after all, "family."

"Come," he commanded quietly, "you must forget Orlov."

Nikolai took Lucy to a house near St. Basil's Cathedral, all barley-sugar towers and domed cupolas, like a castle out of a fairy tale.

Feodor opened the door to them and a servant showed them into a comfortably furnished salon.

"Bring my cousin something to eat and prepare a bed for her will you, Maria?" Nikolai asked. His face was etched with pain and Lucy, who had until that moment, forgotten about his wound, sent Feodor to the kitchen for hot water and clean linen.

"Don't fuss," he said tiredly. "Feodor will do everything that is necessary."

But, nevertheless, he made no demur when Lucy pushed him down into a chair and poured him a glass of wine. He drank it quickly, his face pale in the candlelight. He winced when Lucy eased his coat off his shoulder, protesting that there was no need for her to concern herself.

"Just as there was no need for you to rescue me!" she retorted sharply, trying to stem hurt tears. Couldn't he see that she was trying to make amends, that it would do much to ease her guilty conscience to be allowed to perform this small task, even if Feodor could do it equally well?

His shirt had stuck to the open wound and Lucy was

obliged to soak the fabric very thoroughly before she could pull it away, to disclose a long, angry wound.

Her bowl of water had turned quite red before this task was done and Feodor was sent back to the kitchen to bring fresh.

When she had finished giving instructions as to the need to boil the water and bring clean cloths, Lucy turned her attention to her patient. He was leaning back in the chair, his eyes closed, a faint pulse beating in the livid scar. He looked so exhausted that Lucy's determination almost misgave her. Perhaps she ought to have let Feodor attend him. His touch was probably a good deal more sure than her own.

Nikolai's eyes flickered open. "No need to look so concerned. I am hardly likely to die from a scratch. God, but I'm tired . . ."

"Perhaps you would prefer Feodor to clean the wound," Lucy suggested tentatively. "I'm a little slow and . . ."

"And you have a touch like Angel's wings," Nikolai said drowsily. "If it does not trouble you too much, perhaps you would be kind enough to do it for me. Feodor is more used to doctoring horses than he is men. Besides, he does not smell of lavender and sunshine . . ."

The unexpected compliment caught her off guard. She stared and then flushed, when she saw the amusement lurking in his eyes.

"Blame it on the wine, little cousin. I have had nothing to eat in four-and-twenty hours, and that was grandpère's finest Madeira. It is fortunate that it is not a bullet wound you are attending to, otherwise you would have had to fill me with Vodka, while you removed the bullet, and God knows what effect that would have on me."

His eyes were closing again, and Lucy half suspected that he had no idea what he was saying. When Feodor returned she took the water from him and cleaned the wound thoroughly before applying a pad of linen soaked in spirits, to the torn flesh. Nikolai winced when she pressed it in place but made no other protest; and together she and Feodor managed to achieve a very neat-looking bandage, although, as Nikolai pointed out very dryly, when they had finished, he would now be unable to dress without assistance.

"You have Feodor to perform that service for you," Lucy announced tartly. "And besides it is only for a few days, until the wound starts to heal."

"I am obliged to you," Nikolai said dryly. "Feodor, go and see if Maria has prepared a room for Lucy, will you?"

When the door closed behind Feodor, Nikolai said softly, "I sent him away, because I have something to say to you."

"Is it that we need no longer pretend to be betrothed, now that Vasili is dead?" Lucy asked hesitantly.

Nikolai frowned. "No. Nothing can undo the damage he has already caused. What I wanted to say was . . ." He glanced up as Feodor came back into the room. "It doesn't matter. I have to see the Governor of Moscow tomorrow. Perhaps you would like to come with me? It will give you an opportunity to see the city."

Surprised by this unexpected invitation Lucy paused. It was gradually being borne in upon her that there were few things she would not be happy to do in Nikolai's company. What strange alchemy had been at work within her to have wrought this transformation from hate to . . . love? She tried to suppress the thought, unaware that Nikolai was watching the play of emotions across her face.

"If you would prefer not to, there is no obligation," he began harshly, but Lucy stopped him.

"Oh no! I should like it above all things. That is, if you are sure I shall not be discommoding you?"

She wondered at the bitterness of his laughter, seeing with the eyes of love the taut anger on his face, underlying the mask of exhaustion.

She did love him! How could she not have known it? She savored the knowledge, trying to discover whence this well of feeling sprang; what alien part within herself had first nurtured the seed of that love, but could find no answer.

She could not even decide when hate had first given

way to love or whether it had been there all the time, dormant, waiting for the right moment to burst into painful life. For painful, it most certainly was. Whereas before she could not keep enough distance between herself and her "betrothed," she now found herself wishing that they were in truth promised to marry, that that marriage was the desire of them both, and that Nikolai would seek to take advantage of their present circumstances by curving his arm around her waist, or perhaps placing a kiss on her cheek, or even . . . . but here her wayward thoughts were curtailed. Nothing could be gained from remembering those other moments of intimacy. Those kisses given not in love, but in anger. Kisses that had lingered on in her memory, making her wish that she might, just once, have known the sweetness of Nikolai's lips pressed against her own in love, and not hate.

She lingered beside him unwilling to lose any precious second of his company. Feodor withdrew discreetly, and they were alone.

"Is there something wrong?" Nikolai asked her harshly. He had poured himself another glass of wine and the ruby liquid glowed like fire as he lifted it to his lips. "If it is the memory of a certain event which occurred while we were in the charcoal burners' hut that disturbs you, then it need not. Tonight there is no need for us to share our sleeping hours, and you need not fear that I will subject you to an embrace which you obviously find unpleasant!"

So he *had* known about that kiss! Color washed her pale cheeks. "Please do not talk so," she whispered in stifled accents. "I have wronged you terribly, and you are right to reproach me but . . ."

"Go to bed, Lucy," he said in tired accents. "Otherwise we shall be quarrelling all night, when I would far rather be . . ."

"Sleeping? Of course. Forgive me. You must be exhausted. I shall leave you now."

She paused at the door wondering a little at the derisive smile he gave her.

142

The morning was cold with thin sunshine. Summer was over, Nikolai told her, when she joined him for breakfast. Already the old men in the villages were forecasting an early and hard winter.

Nikolai had removed the sling she had fashioned for him, and in reply to her questions answered curtly that he could manage well enough and that it was, after all, no more than a scratch. Feeling snubbed, Lucy retreated into silence, not venturing another word until Feodor appeared to announce that the captain of the troop was waiting outside to report to Nikolai.

Nikolai excused himself. He was gone nearly an hour and when he returned his face was grim.

"Is something the matter?" Lucy asked tentatively.

"Bonaparte is marching on Moscow. Between Moscow and his army lie our forces, at a small town called Borodino. If General Kutuzov fails to stop the French . . ."

"Do you fear . . ."

"A soldier never fears Lucy," he said harshly. "Now, if you are ready we shall go and pay our respects to the Governor of Moscow."

"It is very kind of you to bother yourself with me in this way . . ."

"My dear Lucy," came the sardonic response, "it is not purely for your benefit. My men are losing heart. I have only a very small force with which to defend this city. If they see me strolling about with my charming bride-to-be, showing her the delights of the town, they are hardly likely to fear that the French are about to arrive at any moment are they? It is all a question of morale, and I must sustain theirs until I know the outcome of Borodino."

Lucy felt too deflated to respond. Castigating herself for being a fool, she allowed Nikolai to escort her to the waiting carriage.

A small group of soldiers outside St. Basil's Cathedral stood to attention, and one or two of them eyed her as they passed. Nikolai noticed and smiled grimly. All good for morale, no doubt, Lucy thought indignantly;

listening with only half an ear while Nikolai told her about the architect who had designed the Cathedral.

"Ivan IV had him blinded when the building work was completed, so that there could never be another Cathedral like it."

Looking at the fantastic formation of its nine towers, Lucy could well believe that there wasn't, but to rob a man of his sight!

"That is Russia for you," Nikolai told her. "This is a cruel land, and it has given birth to a cruel people. Under the veneer of civilization, we are still the savages Europeans delight in calling us behind our backs. That is our heritage."

"And mine."

"Ah yes, but yours is tempered by your father's blood. You have something of his gentleness, I think."

Somehow, he made it sound like a fault. Lucy compressed her lips. Where once such a comment would have driven her to furious protest, she now wanted to beg him to assure her that gentleness or not, he still found her pleasing. A Stanton, she reminded herself firmly, never begged, and certainly not for the love of any cold, proud savage!

Before they called on the Governor, Nikolai showed Lucy the city. She saw the Moskva from high up on the city walls, where it appeared to be no more than a languid blue ribbon of water under the early autumn sun. She saw the old Teremnoy Palace with its state apartments, and the beautiful, breathtaking Iconostasis in the Low Sunday Church, where each precious Icon was set in a frame of gold and the jewelled blues and crimsons of the Icons merged with the smell of incense, so that the two were inseparably intermingled in her mind, for all time.

She had a feeling that it was more than a mere desire to show his men that there was nothing to fear that made Nikolai pause so long before each ancient carving or precious work of art. It was almost as though he were saying "goodbye" to old friends. The thought shivered across her consciousness, making her glance quickly at his shuttered face.

"It is time for me to see the Governor," he said heavily at last. "Come, we don't want to keep him waiting."

"Does he know I shall be with you?"

Nikolai shrugged indifferently. "I have sent him a message to say that I shall be accompanied by my betrothed. He will not find it strange that I should want to combine the business that brings me to Moscow with whatever time I can steal in your company."

Count Rostopchin was a small, plump gentleman who endeavored to conceal the fact that he was beginning to lose his hair by combing what was left of it across his balding pate.

When Lucy and Nikolai were shown in, he was seated with his Countess and his two younger daughters. His sons, he informed Nikolai proudly, were fighting with their Tsar.

Naturally enough this disclosure led to a discussion of the French capture of Smolensk, during which Countess Rostopchin began to weep a little and pray that her sons were both safe. Her daughters, two pretty, dark-haired girls in their early teens, did their best to reassure her, but it was Nikolai who won a rather watery smile with his information that both Alexei and Dimitri had survived the skirmish with the French and were looking forward to their first real battle.

"They are so very young," Count Rostopchin sighed, shaking his head. "But we are grateful to you for bringing us news of them. Perhaps, my dear," he said to his countess, "you would care to take Miss Stanton to your own sitting room for a while so that the Prince and I can discuss our business."

Lucy would have preferred to listen to the gentlemen, but the countess was a kind-hearted soul anxious for all the latest gossip from St. Petersburg and full of promises to call and see the old Prince and Tante Sophy just as soon as her husband could spare a carriage. "My poor husband. He has been quite run off his feet! So many persons coming and going. Will you have another cup of tea? No? Some cake then? What was I saying? Oh yes . . . so many messengers from the Tsar and my poor husband forever having to go out. I can't remember when we last had such a busy summer. Now tell me, my dear, is it true that the very latest designs from France necessitate the dampening of one's skirts so that one can quite plainly see . . ." She broke off to instruct her daughters to go and find their governess, before dropping her voice to a whisper ". . . a lady's body through them?"

I believe some ladies do go to such extremes, "Lucy agreed, suppressing a small smile. "But of course, most do not. I think you will find the style very elegant and graceful. Tante Sophy says it is the most becoming line she has seen in years."

Plainly relieved to discover that she was not expected to dampen her muslins and expose her body to the eyes of the world, the countess settled down for a comfortable coze. It wasn't long before Lucy had an intimate knowledge of the countess's many ailments, a history of her offspring, and an open invitation to call the Rostopchin's home her own whenever she chose.

"I understand that you are recently betrothed to your cousin! Such an excellent match in every way. How pleased the dear Prince must be! If it weren't for this horrid war, I should give a ball to introduce you to Moscow society; but many people have returned to St. Petersburg, and the town has become very flat. When is the marriage to take place?" she asked.

Lucy saw with relief that the gentlemen had come to join them. Nikolai caught the tail-end of the question and answered the appeal in her eyes.

"Not until Grandpère is fully recovered, unfortunately," he responded with a smile in Lucy's direction that sent painful shivers of pleasure along her spine. "I must return Lucy to Tante Sophy for now, but I hope it will not be too long before we all meet again." He raised the Countess's fingers to his lips in a very gallant fashion and then turned to Lucy, drawing her hand through his arm in a manner that brought a sentimental tear to the Countess's eyes.

"Such a charming couple," she remarked to her family when their visitors had gone. "So very well matched in every way." If only her own dear girls could achieve even half such creditable matches, she would be well pleased indeed!

Her husband made a brief response. Truth to tell, his mind was not on the future husbands his daughters might be expected to secure or even the marriage of the young couple who had just left.

He went to the window and stared out at the familiar skyline of Moscow. What the Prince had come to tell him was serious news indeed. Should General Kutuzov fail to defeat the French at Borodino, he was commanded to put Moscow to the torch, to burn down the ancient Kremlin and its walls. In his moment of triumph Bonaparte would know defeat as the city he had expended so much on capturing burned around him. It was a drastic step to take.

The Tsar had sent no more than the men under Prince Nikolai's command to aid him. They faced alone the might of the French Empire. However, one must not look on the black side. Kutuzov was their best general and would undoubtedly defeat the French upstart. Still, one remembered Austerlitz. He excused himself to his wife and went down to his stables to give instructions to his servants. Maybe he could not save Moscow, but he could save his family. At the first sign that the French were on their way, he would send the women folk to his brother's estate.

"Now that my business with the Governor is complete, I shall take you back to Tante Sophy. She will be wondering what has happened."

"Poor Tante Sophy. I only hope she has been able to keep Grandpère from suspecting."

"Don't worry," Nikolai reassured her. "She knows I will bring you back safely."

"They are both so pleased about our 'betrothal' I hate deceiving them like this." Lucy had been following a train of thought of her own, imagining what it would be

147

like if Nikolai and she were really betrothed, and he had saved her from Vasili Orlov. Surely they would not be riding so sedately side by side. She became lost in a delightful dream in which Nikolai was declaring his undying love and was rudely awakened when that same gentleman advised her to have a care for where she was going, otherwise she might well end up in the ditch.

It was early afternoon when they reached the estate. Tante Sophy came running from the house to greet them, anxiety in every line of her body.

"My poor child," she cried, embracing Lucy. "What you must have endured at the hands of that brute. I hope you punished him severely, Nikolai. To dare to snatch Lucy from her grandfather's lands."

"Well, he will never do so again," Nikolai replied dryly as he swung down from his horse to join them.

Tante Sophy looked from Nikolai's bleak face to Lucy's pale one.

"He's dead," Nikolai offered briefly. "And now I'd like a bath and some sleep, in that order. Everything all right with Grandpère?"

"Yes. He was not feeling too well, and when he asked after Lucy I told him she was in her room. How long . . ."

"Today only," Nikolai responded anticipating her question. "I must rejoin my men as soon as I can. The Tsar has instructed me to organize the defense of Moscow, just in case the French get through."

He strode away from them before Tante Sophy could question him further, leaving Lucy feeling not a little forlorn and sorry that their enforced seclusion had come to an end.

She had still not thanked him properly she thought guiltily nor told him how much she regretted all the wild accusations she had hurled at him.

She gave Tante Sophy an edited account of the events of the previous day, reluctant to go into too much detail, and passed on to her Countess Rostopchin's messages.

"Oh, quite the most silly female, but charming, nonetheless. I suspect she will be calling on us before the week is out. Still, it will be company. You may depend upon it, Lucy, she will wish to further the acquaintance-ship. Those daughters of hers will need husbands before too many years are out, and she will be looking to you for your patronage once you are married to Nikolai. I expect by then your own nurseries will be well on the way to being full," she added complacently, checking as Lucy gave a small gasp.

"Is something wrong?"

"No . . . no . . . nothing at all!"

She had just had a momentary vision of a small child with Nikolai's dark hair and green eyes. An enchantingly solemn little boy, or perhaps a tiny, dimpled girl? She tried hard not to let such tormenting images intrude on her hard-won peace of mind.

Despite her protests that she was not tired, Lucy was persuaded to retire to her room and slept until quite late in the afternoon. When she awoke the house was silent. Alarmed, without knowing why, she dressed and ran downstairs.

Tante Sophy was sitting in the salon, sewing.

"Where is Nikolai?" Lucy asked her.

"Gone back to Moscow my dear. He wouldn't let me wake you. He left not five minutes ago."

Lucy flew out of the house and around to the stables where she waited in a fever of impatience while a groom saddled her mare. If she rode through the wood she might be able to catch Nikolai before he had gone too far. She didn't stop to question her burning desire to see him. All she knew was that it was imperative that he did not leave before she had made her apology and they had said good-bye.

The mare's sides were damp, heaving with strain by the time Lucy managed to catch up with her quarry. He wasn't riding particularly fast but the straight line of his back was somehow a warning not to intrude on his privacy. A little daunted Lucy hesitated, but it was too late. He had looked back and seen her.

"Lucy!" His brows drew together in the familiar frown. "What the devil . . ."

"I wanted to say 'good-bye' to you," she blurted out, appalled at her own gaucherie, "and to apologize again for . . . for all the horrid things I said to you."

"As far as the latter is concerned, once was enough and as for the former . . ." He sighed impatiently. "Very well. Why not! Although why I should be tormented in this fashion I cannot conceive," he muttered under his breath, as she drew level with him. "Come, let us make our 'good-byes' then. What a very civilized English custom it is to be sure. Come here!"

Angrily he dismounted and swung Lucy down from her own saddle, holding her against his body.

Lucy raised her face, dismayed by the brooding fury she saw in his eyes.

"By all means, let us be civil," he mocked bitterly, his hands hardening on her shoulders. "Tell me, though, which role is it I am to play on this occasion? Am I to be the maligned cousin or the affectionate lover? Or perhaps since this could be the last time we shall meet, I may be given the choice?"

Shock had robbed her of the power to speak. His manner was so tautly savage, speaking of emotions so entirely beyond her comprehension that Lucy was unable to answer him.

"Very well! Since you say nothing, I shall make my own choice!"

His arms tightened around her, his breath stirring the damp ringlets clustering on her forehead.

"If you can endure my embrace no other way, perhaps you had best close your eyes, and make believe I am Orlov," he said fiercely as his mouth claimed hers, silencing her protest.

It was a kiss of mingled pain and pleasure, igniting within her a need that transcended all other desires she had ever known. Her flesh seemed to melt into Nikolai's, her lips flowering into life beneath the bruising pressure of his. She never wanted the kiss to end. Never wanted to leave the intoxicating warmth of his arms. She forgot that Nikolai did not share the love that was consuming her and sought only to convey the depth and intensity of her feelings for him. It was as though a spell had been woven about her, making everything but the magic of that moment fade into oblivion.

"My God!"

Nikolai thrust her from him, wrenching the frail fabric of her rosy dreams.

"You cared about him that much?" He laughed bitterly. "Goodbye, little cousin. I cannot say that I am glad we have met. Indeed, my life would have been a happier thing had we not, and happier still if you had not forced this last upon me." His mouth twisted. "No man likes to be substituted for another. You would do well to remember that. You must think yourself lucky that I am needed urgently in Moscow, otherwise I might be tempted to immerse myself fully in the role you have thrust upon me, and play Orlov's part to the full. And I do not imagine *he* would have stopped at a few kisses!"

Lucy's lips felt numb. Her whole body seemed to be trembling with the agony his words were causing her.

"Nikolai, I . . ."

"No more apologies," he said curtly. "Go back to Tante Sophy. Good-bye, Lucy."

He did not turn once to look at her, even though she remained standing in the road long after he was a mere speck on the horizon. A terrible bitterness swept through her. She had deluded herself into believing their embrace meant as much to him as it had to her. To him, she was his foolish, unwanted cousin. To her, he was the sole reason for her existence and would be forever more!

Ten

It seemed to Lucy that the days dragged by interminably. There was no word from Nikolai in Moscow; and considering the nature of their parting, she wasn't sure what she would have said to him had he suddenly arrived in their midst.

One blue and gold day gave way to another. The serfs brought in the harvest, and naturally, Lucy was expected to be present at the feast given to celebrate the occasion. Here there was none of the surliness she had been led to expect by the aunts. Indeed she fancied the serfs were better cared for than even the Stanton Lacey tenants. Chubby smiling children clutched at their mother's skirts; sun-tanned men toasted the old Prince and his ladies. The harvest had been a good one and the old Prince reflected soberly later that they were lucky it had not had to be destroyed, as so many others had, to prevent it going to feed the French armies.

Grandpère fretted for news of the War, as Lucy knew, and although she and Tante Sophy did their best to calm him, it was plain to both of them that he was endangering his recovery with his acute anxiety.

"If only there were some way we could find out what was happening," he protested on more than one occasion. "It is more than a sennight since Nikolai told us that the French were to meet our forces at Borodino, and not a word!"

"Nikolai will let us know as soon as he can," Tante

Sophy soothed placidly. "The Tsar has given him an important post; he cannot be forever deserting it to visit us!"

One morning, though, there was news. An excited servant burst in while Tante Sophy and Lucy were still at breakfast to tell them that a carriage had been seen travelling very fast on the road to the house. No one had been able to identify the vehicle, and the ladies had to contain their curiosity with what scant patience they could muster.

It was well over an hour before the carriage came to a halt in the stable yard. Tante Sophy and Lucy both hurried out to greet their unexpected visitors, who turned out to be Countess Rostopchin and her daughters.

Tante Sophy and the Countess embraced.

"No—no tea," said the Countess breathlessly in response to Tante Sophy's invitation. "We cannot stop. We are on our way to my brother-in-law's estate and must make all haste, but I promised my husband I would warn you. Our armies have been defeated at Borodino, and at this very moment the *French Monster* marches on our beloved city! Indeed, he may very well be there even now! I begged my husband to come with us, but he would not. His place is with Prince Nikolai and his men, he claims. As if one more man will make any difference! They are all doomed. How can a single troop hold back an entire army? What can our dearest Tsar be thinking of?"

She broke down in noisy tears, allowing Tante Sophy to lead her into the house, where, despite her protests, she drank two cups of very milky tea and ate several small almond cakes, before regaling them with the remainder of her story.

"You cannot stay here!" she told them. "If Bonaparte takes Moscow it will not be safe. Come with us. I could not rest if I allowed Prince Nikolai's betrothed to be exposed to those French fiends!"

Lucy and Tante Sophy exchanged glances. At all costs this worrying news must be kept from the old Prince. If he knew the danger his grandson faced . . . .

and, Lucy reflected somberly, the danger they themselves might face, if Countess Rostopchin's worst fears were realized . . . he would worry himself into the grave.

"Say you will lose no time in coming with us, I beg you . . ." Countess Rostopchin was pleading, but Tante Sophy managed to soothe her. "You will make yourself ill, my dear," she said firmly. "Think of the example you are setting to your girls! I do not believe Moscow will fall to the French. The Tsar will have some plan up his sleeve, you will see. We shall stay here. I am sure if we were in any danger Nikolai would have found a way to let us know."

Slowly, the little countess allowed herself to be persuaded into a calmer frame of mind, although remaining disturbed at her companions's determination to remain where they were.

Lucy said good-bye to her with mixed feelings, which it seemed Tante Sophy shared.

"If only Nikolai were here, or your grandfather not so frail. I don't know what we ought to do for the best, Lucy," she confessed when they were alone. "It is at times such as these that one most appreciates a gentleman's presence. If the French have entered Moscow, as Countess Rostopchin believes, then we are indeed in some danger. You more than me!"

"If the French are in Moscow, I doubt they will be in any great hurry to leave," Lucy replied stalwartly. "Bonaparte will wish to rest his men; to re-provision his army. If only we knew exactly what the position is!"

The same thought was in both their minds. If they were in danger Nikolai would surely have found a way of warning them . . . Unless, of course, he was no longer able to . . . .

"We could send one of the servants to Moscow . . ." Lucy suggested tentatively, but Tante Sophy shook her head.

"That would not serve, my dear. If Feodor was here . . . but the others are like children. No, we can only wait . . . and hope."

But as Lucy was the first to admit, hers was a nature

that demanded action, not passive patience. All through the long afternoon she roamed restlessly through the house, not daring to go out lest a messenger arrived while she was gone.

The strain upon her and Tante Sophy was so great that by four o'clock the latter was forced to retire to her room with a sick headache.

"Wake me the instant we have any news," was her last command to Lucy before she went upstairs.

Left alone, Lucy could scarcely contain her anxiety. What if Nikolai had been injured . . . or . . . but, no, she would not let herself dwell on such a possibility. The thought, however, would not be denied, and at last unable to bear it any longer, she made up her mind. *She* would go to Moscow!

Before her courage deserted her, she sat down and scribbled a brief note for Tante Sophy, explaining what she was doing. A quick check on grandpère revealed that he was sleeping peacefully. Lucy kissed him lightly on the brow and then tip-toed away to prepare herself for the journey to Moscow.

Lucy elected to ride a stallion that rightly belonged to Nikolai, a huge, black Arab with a wicked temper and rolling eyes, but he was far faster than any other horse in the stables; and, more important, he had the stamina for the double journey that would be required of him.

Even if they made good time, Lucy doubted if she could reach Moscow much before evening, which meant that she would not return until the following morning. It was a daunting thought.

It was not a journey she cared to remember. The stallion was very fresh, sawing on his bit, and wrenching her arms as she struggled to control his pace. If she let him exhaust himself too soon they might never reach Moscow, let alone return!

The sky seemed deep rose and vivid blue by the setting sun when Lucy reached the outskirts of Moscow. From the other side of the Moskva she scanned the silent city. The dying daylight had the curious effect of making the gilded cupolas and towers float in a mirage-like fashion through the evening mist so that the whole city looked as though it could disappear on a breath of wind. Summoning her flagging courage, Lucy rode into the town. Nothing stirred! She rode past the cathedral, empty and vaguely eerie in the cool evening air; past the Granovitia Palace, the ancient home of the Romanovs, her eyes searching the murky alleys for a glimpse of the familiar white and gold uniform, but there was nothing.

It was then that the truth dawned. Moscow was a deserted shell! Its people had crept away like thieves in the night. She shivered, the stallion's hoofbeats echoing loudly on the cobbles. Where was everyone? Where was Nikolai? All at once she felt terribly afraid. On her left was the house to which Vasili Orlov had taken her, but she scarcely glanced at it. The old terrors had given way to newer, sharper ones.

Suddenly she heard voices and checked. Half a dozen men came around the corner, stopping dead at the sight of her. They were wearing the uniform of Napoleon's Grande Armee and the blood drained from Lucy's face as she heard one of them cry, "Look, a woman! A lady by the looks of her! Get her men, a fine prize for Murat! He will pay us well for her. It's been a long time since he'd had a *lady* to warm his bed! . . . A long time since any of us have . . ." he ruminated to the bawdy laughter of his companions.

Lucy wheeled the stallion about, trying desperately to escape, but it was too late. Rough hands grasped her bridle, pulling her rudely from the saddle.

"She's even better than I thought," one of her captors announced. "Young too. Damned if we don't keep her for ourselves! What do you say, men?"

Raucous cheers greeted the suggestion. Lucy had to bite her lip to prevent herself from showing her fear.

"What's going on here?" A broad, swarthy-faced man appeared among them, thrusting the others aside as he came to stand in front of Lucy, feet apart, barrel-chest outthrust.

"The only Russian we've been able to find apart from a few useless peasants, who disappeared before we could question them," responded one of the soldiers. "A fine lot, aren't they? The men run leaving the womenfolk behind to do the fighting, and I dare swear this one knows a bit about that! Pretty ain't she? Wild as a hell-cat I'll be bound. We were just going to bring her to you, Sir!"

Sir! Lucy's heart gave a terrified bound. This must be the "Murat" of whom they had just spoken. One of Bonaparte's most feared generals; a man whose appetites were said to be both catholic and boundless! She was trembling so much that she could hardly stand.

"Your name, girl?"

She ignored the question.

"Tell the general your name!" A vicious twist of her arm forced a small cry from her lips.

"It is Lucy . . . Lucy Stanton . . ." she said proudly, in English.

"English! Wait until Bonaparte knows about this!" An Englishwoman in Moscow. Well, well. I think our Emperor will want to question this young lady. When he has finished with her, you can bring her to my quarters. Take the girl to the antechamber, and if anyone questions you, you can say I sent her. A present for my Emperor!" His ugly face twisted in a mocking grin. "Until later, *ma belle*. Don't look so worried. We shall enjoy ourselves together you and I . . ."

With that threat ringing in her ears, Lucy was dragged away to the palace she had passed only minutes earlier. A captain on guard outside the main doors murmured a sleepy protest, but was overruled as her guards explained the nature of their business.

"Murat sent her? Very well then, but I warn you, you had best not disturb the Emperor. He is sleeping at the moment."

"Sleeping is he?" Several coarse jests were exchanged and then Lucy was escorted to a small antechamber, furnished only with a chair and a table.

"Ought we to place a guard over her?" one of her captors asked the other.

"No, no need," his companion replied. "Where can she go? No, I'm off to get something to eat, and more important, something to drink. They say this vodka is really something! Leave her there. She'll be all right. When the Emperor has finished with her, Murat will make sure she's properly entertained!"

She was alone, frightened and cold, and huddled into her chair. What on earth was she going to do? Her brain seemed incapable of appreciating the enormity of her danger. All that concerned her was that Nikolai must be dead. Harsh sobs shook her body as she thought of her cousin.

Outside the dying sun was turning the earth crimson. It almost looked as though the whole city was on fire. Why if one looked hard enough it was even possible to imagine tendrils of black smoke rising heavenward. Lucy staggered to her feet, rubbing her tired eyes. Moscow was on fire! Moscow was burning!

The guard burst into the room. Completely ignoring Lucy, he banged on the inner door as she stepped back into the shadows. "Warn the Emperor," he shouted. "The city is on fire!"

Lucy could hear the sound of running feet in the passage outside. No one seemed to be paying the slightest bit of attention to her. She hurried through the door and out into the street. Thick black smoke made it almost impossible to breathe. If only she knew where they had taken her horse! Soldiers rushed through the streets, shouting instructions to one another, as they sought to contain the confusion. Lucy hurried down a narrow street that seemed to lead toward the river, hoping to find a way out of the city. She was hopelessly lost! Tears caused by the choking smoke streamed from her eyes, and all around her were crackling flames.

Somehow, she managed to find her way back to St. Basil's but found no sign of any soldiers or her horse. A fit of coughing overcame her, and when she recovered, she realized that her surroundings were vaguely familiar. She could see the shape of the city walls through the billowing smoke. Hope stirred. Surely Nikolai's house was not far from here.

She found it several minutes later. But when she

pushed open the door, her last hopes died. The house was empty! An empty glass stood on a table in the salon, a bottle of wine uncorked beside it, as though whoever had been drinking it had left quickly. Lucy closed her eyes, silent tears rolling down her cheeks. An ominous puff of black smoke in the hallway warned her that it was time to leave. She hurried to the door, falling back in alarm as she saw the flames licking greedily around the hall. A blazing spar crashed down from the ceiling blocking her exit.

Lucy searched desperately for some means of escape; all around her the old wooden building took fire from the burning spar. The heat was overpowering, driving her back into the salon. A neighboring house collapsed before her eyes as the flames devoured it. This was the end. She could never survive this burning pyre. She closed her eyes and prayed that when the end came, it would be mercifully swift and that she would never feel the cruel caress of the flames against her skin.

As she was sucked down into the dark vortex of nothingness, waiting to claim her, she gave a final passionate cry. Nikolai's name was the last word on her lips as consciousness fled.

"We have done it, Nikolai! The French are in utter confusion!"

"But at what cost?" Nikolai commented soberly to his second-in-command.

Both of them were dressed in unappealing rags, dirt smeared over their faces, their hair unkempt—a far cry from the uniform normally adopted by the Tsar's personal Regiment.

"You had no choice," the young lieutenant reminded him. "It was the Tsar's order."

But it was an order that may never have been given had he not put the idea in the Tsar's mind, Nikolai reflected soberly. The moment that news of the Russian defeat at Borodino reached Moscow, he had been waiting for Napoleon's arrival. With Count Rostopchin's aid they had cleared the city, and then his small troop had set to work carefully baiting the well-laid trap. Now they had sprung it, but as he had so lately remarked, at what cost? Moscow was burning, and their attempts to repel the French could well mean the death of the city for all time!

Knowing that his small troop could never hold off the French in a direct confrontation, Nikolai had instructed them to disguise themselves as peasants—the more sullen and lack-witted the better, so that they could attack their enemy in the same deadly fashion that a horse-fly did its prey. So far their tactics had been overwhelmingly successful. They had emptied the city of food, but had left ample supplies of vodka conspicuously on view. Now the fires were splitting the French forces into small, panic-stricken bands.

A young ensign came rushing up to the ramshackle barn Nikolai had made his Headquarters, his face flushed with triumph.

"We've captured some of their horses, Sir. Alexei is bringing them in."

"Good." Nikolai approved. "That will prevent them leaving the city to raise the alarm among the troops encamped to the North of us. You'd better bring the animals in here. We've kept the barn thoroughly doused with water and so it should be quite safe from the fire. The moment the French start to flee, I want you to be ready to start putting the fires out. We want to do as little damage as possible."

The two young ensigns brought in their prizes, not without some difficulty, for the horses had been panicked by the flames and smoke. One in particular appeared to be giving them trouble, his high-pitched screams of rage cutting across Nikolai's instructions.

"Can't someone control that animal?" he asked wearily, getting up to see what was going on.

"It's this damned Arab stallion, Sir," the ensign explained. "I've never seen such a horse. I wonder who he belongs to?"

To his second-in-command's amazement Nikolai pushed the ensign aside, grasping the stallion's reins and running expert hands along his heaving flanks.

"Where did you find this horse?" he asked curtly.

"Outside the Palace. Some of Murat's men had been trapped inside. We've taken them prisoner."

"Bring them in here, I want to talk to them," Nikolai commanded. "Now!"

As the ensign disappeared into the smoke-filled gloom, Nikolai explained brusquely to his second-in-command, "That horse is mine. It was stabled on the Kuragin Estate."

"Perhaps your family sent a servant to Moscow for news," the lieutenant suggested.

Nikolai shook his head. He was standing next to the stallion and he pointed to the short stirrups and long reins.

"No. Look at these. Whoever rode the horse was either a boy, or a woman! Can you take command for me?"

Just as he gave his assent, the ensign returned with half a dozen ragged looking French soldiers.

Under Nikolai's questioning they admitted that they were Murat's men and had become separated with the rest of their troup. Nikolai then demanded to know how the black stallion had come into their possession.

"The English girl you mean?" croaked one of the soldiers, ignoring the venomous looks his captain was giving him. "Murat sent her to the Emperor, but then the fires broke out and all hell was let loose."

"And none of you saw her after that?"

They all shook their heads.

"Take them away," Nikolai commanded grimly.

When they had gone he turned to his lieutenant. "My cousin," he explained briefly. "God knows why she came to Moscow in the first place, but I have to find her. I'll take a couple of the men with me."

He was gone before the young lieutenant could protest, disappearing into the flame-filled night.

Nikolai had picked the two young ensigns to accompany him. Both of them had overheard him questioning the French soldiers, and the younger of the two asked him uncertainly, "What do you intend to do, Sir? Search the Palace area?"

Nikolai shook his head decisively. "No, if my cousin

did escape from the Palace, I think I know where she would go. I can only pray to God that I am right and that we are in time."

Through the red, burning mist, Lucy thought she heard someone calling her name. Reluctantly she opened her eyes.

"Lucy?"

A man was standing over her, dressed in tattered rags, his face blackened from the smoke.

"Lucy, it's me!" the grimy stranger said impatiently. "Nikolai!"

"Nikolai?" Lucy stared at him in disbelief. "But you're dead! The French killed you, and now I'm going to die, too." She shivered, choking on the acrid smell of burning wood.

"Don't be so foolish," came Nikolai's acid comment.

Nothing could have been more calculated to snap Lucy out of her apathy. It *was* Nikolai, she thought joyfully, struggling to her feet.

Above them she heard a sudden warning shout. There was a shower of sparks and then a crash. A burning pain shot through her ankle.

Nikolai swore. "Can you move Lucy?"

She tried to wriggle free of the heavy beam, but she was trapped, the pain in her ankle excruciating. Bravely she tried not to let Nikolai see how terrified she was.

"I think I'm trapped," she said shakily. "You had better go, Nikolai. No sense in both of us . . . ."

"Nothing is going to happen to either of us," Nikolai interrupted firmly. "Just as long as we both keep calm. My men have gone for water to damp down the fire. Once they've done that, we can lift that beam off you. What are you doing in Moscow anyway?"

Lucy explained to him about Countess Rostopchin's visit, trying to ignore the gentle probing of his fingers as they examined her injured ankle.

"I think you've broken it," he pronounced when his examination was finished. "I'll try to lift this spar off you, so that I can get a better look at it."

Lucy fainted twice during the time it took Nikolai

to remove the spar. Her ankle had begun to throb unbearbly, and if it hadn't been for the cool draught of fresh air blowing in off the river she was sure they must have choked to death on the smoke. Nikolai's men had returned and were trying to put out the flames. One of them helped Nikolai lift the beam, while another gently pulled her out from beneath it.

When they went back to work, putting out the fires, Nikolai removed his tattered jacket. Underneath he was wearing his own shirt, now filthy, but still a good deal more respectable than the rags he had assumed as a disguise. He took off his shirt and ripped it down the front using the fabric to bind Lucy's ankle.

"I'm going to try to set the bones," he warned her. "It will be painful, but better now than later."

Lucy gritted her teeth, unable to tear her eyes away from the skilled hands working so efficiently to ease her pain. Nikolai kept up a flow of small talk, telling her how he had come to learn of her presence in Moscow and her subsequent capture.

"But . . . how . . . did . . . you manage to find me?" Lucy bit out painfully.

"Luck . . . and instinct. There were only two places in Moscow that you knew—one of them I didn't think you would ever want to see again, and so I chose the other. Hold tight, now child."

He made a sudden deft movement, and there was a pain like nothing Lucy had ever dreamed existed, like lightning flashing across the sky, gone almost before she had time to experience it, leaving a delicious sensation of relief.

"Lucy, don't faint on me now," Nikolai said tersely above her. "It won't be much longer. I'll just rebind your ankle, and then we'll be out of here. We've even been able to recover my stallion. You don't believe in doing things by halves do you?" he asked grimly. "Didn't you realize he was half savage? He could have thrown you . . . trampled on you . . ."

"But if he had, I'm sure you would have been there to rescue me." Lucy heard herself say drowsily. "You always are. This is the third time you've saved me, Nikolai . . ."

She was floating away on a golden cloud. Nikolai's arms were supporting her, carrying her away from the blazing building, and out into the cold, clean night air. All around her she could hear the deep rumble of male voices, the occasional terse command punctuated by short silences. She gave a faint sigh and turned into the protection of Nikolai's arms.

The next thing she knew she was mounted before Nikolai on his stallion. Although her ankle was still throbbing it was not nearly so painful as it had been. For some reason she felt a great longing to pretend that she had not recovered consciousness, so that she might enjoy the security of Nikolai's embrace a little longer, but this was not to be. She must have made some small, betraying movement; because when she looked up, he was watching her with a grim expression in his eyes. She remembered the inferno from which he had rescued her and started to shudder convulsively.

"You could have been killed," she whispered tremulously. "How could you have risked your own life to save mine?"

"How could I not, and still call myself a man?"

"That is the third time," Lucy murmured, unaware that she was repeating herself.

"Perhaps I ought to claim a forfeit then," Nikolai said dryly. "We have a saying in our country that he who saves another's life on three occasions shall merit the right to call that life his own. Would you be willing to pay such a forfeit?"

The awful blackness was reaching out to claim her again, and that must be why she had imagined the curious look of intensity in Nikolai's eyes.

She tried to tell him that her life was his to do with as he willed, but somehow the words were never formed. There was only darkness and silence . . . . and the red-hot burning pain of her ankle.

Eleven

Lucy was unconscious when Nikolai carried her into the house. Tante Sophy, beside herself with anxiety listened as he explained all that had happened, all the while, wringing her hands over her grand-niece's state.

"She will soon recover," Nikolai said brusquely, but Tante Sophy was not convinced.

"This was not some mere fall from a horse, or something of that order," she chided him.

In the days that followed, her worst fears were realized. Lucy sank deep into unconsciousness, tormented by nightmares, alternately feverish and shivering. Only Nikolai's presence seemed to have the power to soothe her, and it was he who told Tante Sophy that Lucy was to be told nothing of those dreadful dreams, when they had feared for her reason as she confused Vasili Orlov with the French soldiers and lived through her ordeal over and over again.

A doctor summoned hastily from a neighboring estate pronounced a severe case of brain fever and advised complete rest until the patient started to recover. For Nikolai's impromptu handling of her broken ankle he had somewhat grudging praise and allowed that, with luck, the young lady would be walking again by Christmas, and without any trace of a limp.

"Purely by good luck of course," he added with a reproving glare for Nikolai. "As for the nightmares—in time they will fade. The young have remarkable powers of recuperation."

Gradually Lucy started to recover. Tante Sophy adhering to her nephew's command, told her only that she had suffered a severe fever following her return from Moscow, but was now well on the way to full recovery.

Grandpère spent an hour with her one afternoon, shortly after the doctor had pronounced her well enough to have visitors, provided she was not over-excited; and it was from him that Lucy learned that Moscow had not been as badly damaged as had first been feared.

Her second piece of news concerning the war came from Nikolai himself, who had come to see her at Tante Sophy's insistence.

"The child is fretting for you Nikolai. I believe she wishes to thank you for your timely rescue."

She has already thanked me enough," was his curt response, but nevertheless when Maria, Lucy's maid, took her mistress her afternoon tea, she found the two cousins together.

Nikolai had only just arrived. He didn't sit down, choosing instead to stand by the window with his back to Lucy. His stance had a depressing effect on her already over-strained nerves. It seemed that he wanted neither her thanks nor her company. She stifled a small sigh and wondered why it was that she was condemned to endure this unwanted love.

"As soon as you are sufficiently recovered, you will be returning to St. Petersburg," Nikolai informed her when Maria had gone.

Lucy already knew this. Tante Sophy had been full of plans for their departure only that morning. Apparently the Tsar was planning a hectic round of festivities for the coming winter, to celebrate their retention of Moscow. It was rumored that the French were retreating, unable to support themselves on the ravished land behind them and unwilling to march farther into Russia, with winter ahead of them.

There was one item of news which Tante Sophy had not told her, though. She was leaving that to Nikolai.

166

"Will you be coming with us?" Lucy asked her cousin. She picked unhappily at her coverlet, unable to bear the cold rejection she was sure she would see in his eyes, if she lifted her head.

"No," he answered curtly. "I have duties that keep me in Moscow. Lucy, if you are well enough, there are matters we must discuss."

Her eyes flew to his face.

"This business of our betrothal. It seems Grandpère intends to give a ball when you are well enough to announce the date of our marriage!"

Her throat felt oddly constricted.

"But we are not going to be married. Our betrothal is not real . . . you said that . . ." She faltered into silence, wishing she was able to divine what he was thinking.

"Circumstances have changed since then," Nikolai said abruptly. "Not in our feelings toward each other of course—nothing has changed there . . ."

If only he knew how wrong that statement was, Lucy thought in anguish. But of course, she could never tell him, never divulge by so much as a glance or a gesture just how radically *her* feelings had changed—not while his remained the same.

"However, I have been thinking," Nikolai continued, "A marriage between us would perhaps be no bad thing, certainly it would be no worse than many another, and it would give Grandpère a great deal of pleasure. I give you my word that I shall not . . . ."

"Stop it. Stop it!" Lucy put her hands over her ears. "I wanted to marry for love . . ."

Her anguish broke through the control she was trying to place on herself. Nikolai abandoned his stance by the window and came over to the bed.

"I should have thought Orlov taught you enough about 'love' to make you realize that it is a bitter, destructive emotion, and that you are better off without it!"

He was quite right. However, it wasn't Vasili who had taught her the agony of unrequited love, but himself!

"You still haven't given me an answer, Lucy," Nikolai reminded her. "And think carefully before you do. Remember, a marriage between us would make Grandpère very happy . . ."

"Then why not?" Lucy said bitterly. "Let us by all means make *someone* happy, even if we cannot be ourselves!"

Nikolai's eyes darkened to deepest jade, as stormy as wind tossed seas.

"Would you be so uncaring were it Orlov's proposal you were accepting, I wonder? Or would you expect a more demonstrative token than mere words?"

As he spoke he bent over her, imprisoning her hands within his own, his mouth parting hers in a kiss of bitter anger, which punished rather than pleased.

For a second her lips quivered betrayingly beneath the pressure of his, and then she had herself under control. If they were to be married she must learn to guard her feelings well. This could be the first lesson.

"I should not have done that," he said curtly as he withdrew from her. "Forgive me!"

"For what? Kissing me? I dare say I shall have to become accustomed to your kisses—and worse!"

She shrank under the fury leaping to life in his eyes, but it was quickly checked, only his clenched fists betraying the effectiveness of her gibe.

"If you are in agreement we shall be married one month after our betrothal is announced," he said curtly as he left the room.

He might have been asking her to affix her name to some dry legal contract, Lucy thought resentfully, glaring at the closed door. But then, of course, that's all their marriage was to him—a contract!

They reached St. Petersburg before the first frosts. By the end of the month they heard that the French were in retreat, the once-proud army perishing by the thousands as the cold weather and lack of food accomplished what the Russian soldiers could not. Men returning on leave from their regiments reported that the French were dying as they marched ill-equipped and under-nourished to face the reality of a Russian winter.

The snow came early. By mid-November it lay across St. Petersburg like a thick blanket, and already the Neva was frozen.

Lucy's ankle had completely mended, and only a slight weakness lingered as a reminder of what she had endured. Even so, Tante Sophy worried that she looked far too pale, far too wan, for a girl about to celebrate her betrothal.

Only in the sanctuary of her own room could Lucy escape from the preparations. She envied Nikolai, on duty with his regiment, able to escape the constant reminders of their marriage. Such an empty sham, Lucy thought, one afternoon as she contemplated the portrait of her Mama hanging on her bedroom wall. *She* would have understood Lucy's present dilemma! It was not as though she was really breaking her vow, Lucy thought disconsolately. After all she *was* marrying for love, even though the object of that love did not return her feelings.

She was to wear a new gown for the ball. White muslin, embroidered with lovers's knots and small bunches of flowers. It was quite enchanting, but Lucy almost hated it. Grandpère had had a suite of rooms prepared for them, and every day Lucy was expected to go and exclaim over the progress being made in their decoration.

As the month drew on Tante Sophy began to fret that Nikolai would not return from duty in time for the ball. Grandpère soothed her fears.

"Not be here for his own betrothal! Nonsense! I expect he's keeping out of the way of all the fuss, eh Lucy?"

She responded with a forced smile.

The Tsar was back in St. Petersburg. Lucy had seen him drive past in his troika one day while she was out shopping with Tante Sophy. It was rumored that he had brought his sister back with him, and that the two were often closeted together for hours on end in his private chambers. Some people said that the bond between the Tsar and the Grand Duchess was far greater than that between the Tsar and the Tsarina. Lucy wondered if the Tsarina ever got lonely and wished that she were married to a less important personage. There were no children of the marriage, nor likely to be any. Lucy shivered. What sort of marriage would her own be? It was something she no longer wanted to contemplate. Part of her longed to believe in the daydreams that suggested that with intimacy love might come. Another part wondered if the torment of having Nikolai as a husband, but not a lover would be such that she would wish she had never entered into the marriage.

The realization that in the excitement of all the preparations for the ball, she had forgotten to order herself a new gown, sent Tante Sophy hurrying off to see her modiste. Lucy went with her. The two ladies soon became deeply engrossed in comparing two fabrics, and Lucy, losing interest, wandered into the snowy street.

Thick flakes of snow floated earthward, from a pearl gray sky. Lucy walked aimlessly toward the Moika Canal which was situated near the shop. She remembered nostalgically the previous winter, when she had gone skating there with a laughing crowd of other young people. She had been free from the problems that now beset her.

Like a ghost conjured up by her thoughts a figure materialized in front of her. Lucy hesitated, recognizing Anna, but it was too late to pretend she had not seen the other woman.

The vivacity Lucy had so much admired had gone. In its place Anna's face had grown hard and bitter.

"Well might you turn from me," she hissed. "You, who murdered my poor brother!"

Lucy glanced desperately over her shoulder, wishing she had not strayed so far from the shop, but there Tante Sophy had not emerged from the modiste's.

"I am sorry about your brother's death," she replied gravely. "But I cannot pretend to wholly regret it. He would have done me a great harm had my cousin not stopped him!"

"By marrying you! You call that a 'great harm,'" Anna mimicked savagely. "And yet you do not object to marrying your cousin, do you? You would have been better off with Vasili my dear," she said softly. "But I think you know that, don't you? Nikolai does not love you. He is not capable of love. He is a man of ice. I should know. Why do you think I took a lover? I can see him now, your proud cousin. I had thought him safely out of the way at Gatchina, but he was not. He came storming into my room, as cool as you please . . . not to challenge my lover to a duel. Oh no! That would have been completely beneath him! No, all he wished to do was inform me that henceforward, our betrothal was no more!"

Lucy said nothing, but her expression gave her away.

"You love him, don't you?" Anna taunted. "You might just as well love a piece of marble, my dear. Don't think he won't discover your childish devotion, for he will. He will use your love to bind you to him, knowing it will ensure your fidelity, without putting him to the tiresome necessity of ensuring it by other means," she said cruelly. "I shall look forward to your marriage, for I cannot think of a more fitting revenge for my poor Vasili! That cold pride will destroy you my dear, be warned by what I say!"

Lucy was shivering when she had gone, but not from cold. She was very much afraid that Anna had spoken the truth!

She was so subdued on the way back, that Tante Sophy was driven to question her, asking if she felt quite well. Lucy replied listlessly that she was merely a little tired.

Several days after her brush with Anna, Lucy had an idea. It came to her one morning as she was reading a letter from Aunt Phoebe. She would not go through with the marriage, she decided suddenly. She dared not for her pride's sake. No, what she must do was return to England. But how to achieve this?

The problem occupied her thoughts for two whole days, before an unexpected solution presented itself to her in the shape of one of Tante Sophy's friends.

Tante Sophy had taken Lucy with her on a visit to Countess Borsino. The countess began telling Lucy about her nephew who was in London attached to the Russian Embassy. Lucy listened politely, remembering the kindness of the Russian ambassador, in what now seemed like another lifetime.

"My son goes to join his cousin in London in a month's time," the countess added. "Perhaps you would care to entrust to him any messages you might have for your family?"

Lucy was on the point of declining when a sudden, daring thought struck her. She hesitated, and then plunged ahead.

"If you are sure your son will not mind?"

"But of course not. I shall send for him right away."

Ten minutes later, Lucy was being introduced to a rather embarrassed young man, whose smile was engagingly complimentary. When the two older ladies resumed their conversation, he confided to Lucy that he was greatly looking forward to his visit to London.

"I did want to join the Guards," he confessed. "But mama was against it because of the war."

Lucy sympathized with him, wondering how best to steer the conversation in the direction she wished, before her courage deserted her entirely.

"The Tsar's regiment is back in St. Petersburg," the young man was saying. "I saw Prince Nikolai at the Winter Palace only yesterday. What I wouldn't have given to be with him in Moscow! They say the Tsar intends to decorate him for his achievements there."

Lucy felt pain stir deep inside her, and any doubts about the wisdom of the step she was contemplating fled. Nikolai was back in St. Petersburg and yet had made no attempt to see her—his "affianced bride." Her mind was made up. She must leave before her own feelings made it impossible for her to do so.

"I was wondering," she began hurriedly, cutting across her young companion's remarks, "a . . . a friend of mine is wishing to travel to London and has no one to escort her . . . . I was wondering if she might travel with you? For family reasons she does not wish to make her journey public . . . for . . . for a very particular reason . . . ."

There was growing consternation in the young man's eyes. "I hadn't planned on travelling with anyone. Just myself and my manservant."

"This . . . this friend of mine will be no trouble. She is most anxious to reach London. A relative of hers is very ill . . ." Lucy improvised wildly. "Indeed, fatally ill, and she must see him."

The young count's eyes went desperately to his mama, but she was serenely oblivious to his plight.

"Please say you will aid my friend," Lucy begged. "I promise you, you will not regret it!"

He loosened his neckcloth a trifle as though he found it slightly constricting. "Er . . ." He hesitated and Lucy pounced.

"Oh you will! Thank you so much! When do you depart? Please give me all the details so that I may convey them to my friend. She will be so grateful to you."

"I planned to leave at the end of the month," was the strangled reply, "but . . ."

"It is all decided then," Lucy interrupted firmly. "You must come to our ball, and we can complete the arrangements then."

Feeling rather dazed, the young Count heard himself agreeing. "Will your friend be attending?" he asked Lucy.

For a moment she was nonplussed. Then she rallied. "My friend. Oh no . . . she does not go abroad very much, but if you will give me the date and time of your departure she will undertake to be there . . ."

When the visitors had gone the young man sought out his sister, who although still in the schoolroom, was reputed to have a sensible head on her shoulders. She heard him out in silence and then said sagaciously, "There is only one thing for it, Dimitri, you must seek out the Prince and lay the whole before him. You mark my words, it is almost bound to be an elopement!"

Her brother gaped. "An elopement. But how can it be . . . I cannot tell Prince Nikolai that . . . I cannot!"

"You must," his sister told him firmly. "He will be forever indebted to you and compel Mama to allow you to join the regiment . . . you must wait and see."

This dazzling prospect was sufficient to send him hurrying from the house in the direction of the Winter Palace, mentally rehearsing the coming interview, as he went. He tracked down his quarry in an antechamber off the Tsar's office and inquired a little nervously if the Prince might spare him a few minutes.

Nikolai had been waiting for nearly two hours to see the Tsar. His business in Moscow was nearly at an end and he had brought for Alexander several reports on the condition of the retreating French army. He had ridden past them on his way to St. Petersburg and had been filled with pity by what he had seen. Perhaps he was getting old, he thought drearily, as he looked into the eager, young face before him, but war had lost its lustre.

"Sit down," he said to Dimitri, pushing a chair toward him, and wondering what had brought him so summarily into his presence.

Half an hour later, his face growing more shuttered with every hesitant sentence, he knew.

"You did well to come to me," he praised. "Your sister strikes me as a very astute young woman. You will naturally not speak of this matter to anyone . . . for the sake of my cousin's friend's reputation, but I assure you that you can safely leave everything in my hands."

"And Miss Stanton?" Dimitri stammered nervously. "She will expect me to furnish her with details of my journey."

"Yes, of course. Now here is what I suggest you do . . . ."

They parted on terms of extreme affability, so much so that Dimitri was emboldened to ask his new hero if he did not agree that a season spent in London in a stuffy Embassy could in no way compare with life as a member of the Tsar's Regiment.

174

Stifling a small smile Nikolai adroitly pointed out that the Tsar's Regiment was at that moment about to be sent to Moscow to harry the French and was likely to pass an extremely dull winter. London, on the other hand, was reputed to be the home of the most attractive young ladies to be found anywhere in the world. For that reason alone, he suggested, it must surely be worth a visit. He further gilded the lily by pointing out the advantages of a little worldly experience to any young man desirous of making his way in the Tsar's army, and his new friend took his leave of him in far better spirits than those with which he had sought him out.

Left alone in the antechamber, Nikolai wrote a short note, which he left on the table before quitting the room. When one of the Tsar's aides came to summon him to the Tsar's presence, he found the room empty, save for the hastily penned note. The Tsar perused it quickly and smiled. "It seems the frost is not as severe as I thought," he remarked perplexingly to his aide, who later reported to his fellows that the strain of the conflict with the French had affected the Tsar's mind.

Lucy was sitting in the library trying to compose a suitable letter of explanation to grandpère and Tante Sophy when Nikolai strode in. The waste paper basket already bore silent witness to the arduous nature of this task. Thus far she was no further than a rather muddled explanation, which even she herself was having difficulty making sense of!

When she saw Nikolai bearing down upon her, she sprang up, hastily crumpling up her latest attempt to set down her reasons for taking "French Leave" of the dearest, kindest relatives anyone had ever had, and gazed at her cousin with an extremely guilty expression.

"Do I disturb you?" Nikolai asked smoothly. "Forgive me, I had not realized you were busy."

"I am merely writing a letter," Lucy exclaimed in extremely flustered accents.

"A letter?" Nikolai gave her a rather enigmatical smile. "To one of your aunts in England, I suppose?"

175

Lucy eyed him hesitantly, not recognizing him in this unfamiliar suave mood.

"Yes," she agreed at length, hoping she would be forgiven the lie. After all it was not strictly an untruth, for she was writing to an aunt, although not one of the ones he meant!

"I didn't know you were back in St. Petersburg," she commented untruthfully as the silence stretched. Nikolai was regarding the overflowing wastepaper basket with an extremely thoughtful frown. She held her breath, praying that he would not take it into his head to make a closer inspection of its contents.

"No?" Nikolai queried, lifting his eyes to her flushed face. "You surely didn't expect me to miss my own betrothal celebrations? I would have been here sooner, but I had business with the Tsar."

"Business?"

"I have decided to sell out of the regiment. As a family man, I shall not have the time to devote to it that I had in the past. Besides, with Grandpère ailing I need more time to give to running the estates. Shall you like that, do you suppose, having me constantly under your feet?"

Thoroughly unnerved by his continued scrutiny of the paper basket, Lucy stammered some appropriate reply, or at least she thought it appropriate until his eyebrows rose questioningly.

"You will? Strange," he mused. "I had the distinct impression that you would have preferred to keep as great a distance between us as possible. Tante Sophy tells me that she took you to visit Countess Borino, the other day?"

Lucy's heart was pounding like a drum.

"Er . . . yes . . ." She couldn't bring herself to meet his eyes lest he read the truth in them. If only he would take her in his arms and tell her that he never wished to let her go! A wistful smile played around her mouth. If wishes were horses then beggars would ride, so Nanny had been fond of saying. Trite but how true!

"You look thoughtful," Nikolai commented. "Is anything wrong?"

Lucy jumped nervously. If only he would go away and cease tormenting her!

"Wrong? What could be wrong? I am the happiest creature alive!"

"Well, you certainly don't look it," came the dampening response. "There is no need to put on an act for my benefit, Lucy. I am quite aware of your feelings!"

Her heart seemed to have lodged somewhere in her throat. She glanced sharply at Nikolai, wondering if the words contained some hidden meaning. Did he know of her love for him? His face told her nothing, as smooth and unreadable as stone—or ice—she thought bitterly. But surely if he *had* guessed that she loved him, he would never mention it to her.

She had suffered indifference and even anger at his hands, but never deliberate unkindness. He did not have the nature to inflict pain purely for the pleasure of doing so. There was nothing mean about Nikolai. And yet, as Anna had warned her, her love for him gave him an undoubted advantage over her.

"My feelings, whatever they are, are none of your concern!" She forced herself to adopt her old challenging pose, daring him to deny her assertion.

He did not. He eyed her consideringly for a few seconds and then said finally, "Very well. If that is what you wish. I take it I can promise myself the pleasure of at least one waltz with you at the ball?"

His tone puzzled Lucy. She shrugged feigning indifference.

"As many as you wish. After all it is your right . . . now that we are formally betrothed."

"My right. How generous of you to remind me. I hope I shall find you equally obliging when it comes to my other 'rights.' Somehow or other I had expected better from you, Lucy. What happened to the girl who claimed she would only marry for love?"

"Perhaps she grew up," Lucy said sadly.

For a moment she thought Nikolai was going to make a move toward her, but then he checked and strode out of the room, leaving her prey to a desolation that exceeded anything she had ever known before.

Twelve

Lucy prepared for the ball in a mood of intense depression, which she told herself was quite ridiculous, since the decision to leave St. Petersburg was her own, and no one else's; and being the right and only sensible thing to do, should certainly not give rise to the unhappiness which constantly beset her nor the unworthy inclination to abandon her plans and take what the gods were offering.

As she had done for the Tsar's ball, she was wearing the gold and sapphire necklace again, but this time she had another ornament—Nikolai's ring!

In her reticule was the letter she had written to grandpère and Tante Sophy, explaining her reasons for leaving St. Petersburg. There was a hollow sensation in the pit of her stomach as she contemplated their reception of her missive. Sitting waiting for Maria to put the last touches to her appearance, she heard the sound of the first arrivals, and her heart started to beat a little faster. Would Dimitri Borino keep his promise to advise her of the final arrangements for his departure?—*their* departure, she reminded herself bleakly.

The Tsar and his sister had graciously accepted an invitation to attend the ball, and as the first strains of the Polonaise floated through the newly decorated ballroom, Lucy found herself in the Tsar's arms while Nikolai took the Grand Duchess in his.

The Tsar was an admirable dancer, Lucy did not doubt, but she could not stop her eyes straying constantly to that other couple. Nikolai so darkly handsome in his uniform, his smile so much warmer for the Grand Duchess than it ever was for herself. The Tsar was considered to be an exceptionally good-looking man indeed, but in Lucy's mind there was no doubt at all about which of the two gentlemen circling the floor, should be awarded the palm. Unconsciously she gave a small sigh. It was a novel experience for the Tsar of all Russia not to have the complete attention of any female whom he favored with his presence. His eyes twinkled a little. "You are not very flattering, Miss Stanton," he reproached teasingly. "Obviously, you would prefer to be in my sister's place."

Lucy's evident confusion served only to increase his amusement.

"I have long wondered who would melt the ice in which my proud friend has embedded himself. You will find him a good husband, I think. I trust you return his affections? I should not wish to see Nikolai condemned to a loveless marriage. That is a very bitter thing for a man to have to endure."

For a moment his face was shadowed and Lucy guessed that he was thinking of his own marriage. There was only one thing worse than a loveless match, she thought bleakly, and that was one where one loved too much and the other not at all. All doubts fled about her decision to leave. For Nikolai's sake as much as her own, she could not burden him with her unwanted love.

The music stopped. Nikolai relinquished the Grand Duchess and came to claim his dance. It was both Heaven and Hell to be held in his arms, as the haunting strains of a waltz filled the room. His hand on her waist was exactly as impersonal as it ought to be. His steps kept the requisite distance between them. If only he could clasp her a little tighter, hold her as though he never wished to let her go, Lucy thought despairingly. If only she had not been foolish enough to fall in love with him!

"You seem a trifle distraught," Nikolai commended at length. "Perhaps your ankle has not recovered as well as it might?"

"No . . . no . . . it does not trouble me at all!"

"Well, something does! That is the fourth time you have looked toward the doors. Is it a particular person you look for, or is it merely that my company bores you to such an extent that you cannot wait to be free of it?"

In point of fact, Lucy had been looking for Dimitri, but she could hardly tell Nikolai that!

"Your company does not bore me," she replied a little wildly. "How could that be so when . . . when we are to be married?"

"Very easily I should imagine," came the dry retort. "Boredom in marriage seems to be the *derniere cri* these days, or hadn't you noticed? Perhaps you are hoping Vasili Orlov will rise from the dead to rescue you at the eleventh hour in true romantic fashion?"

Lucy went pale at his reference to Vasili, reminding her as it did of Anna and what she had told her. All at once the torment of being so close to Nikolai in body and yet so far apart from him in spirit was too much to be borne. With a small cry, she tore herself from his arms. At that precise moment the music stopped, signalling the end of the dance. She didn't glance back to see if Nikolai was following her, but her hurried flight from the ballroom was impeded by a footman who handed her a note which he had been given, with instructions to pass to her, and her alone.

With a pounding heart Lucy opened it, and read the message it contained. It was from Dimitri, saying that he was waiting for her in the library—with the information she required for her friend!

A little nervously, Lucy made her way to that room, wondering why Dimitri could not have sought her out in the ballroom.

He was standing by grandpère's desk when she opened the door, dressed not in evening clothes, but for travel.

"Miss Stanton!" He was plainly relieved to see her. If anything Lucy thought, he was more nervous than she was herself.

"Thank goodness you are come! I am here to tell you that I leave St. Petersburg tonight. A sudden change in my plans," he explained as Lucy's eyes widened in shocked surprise.

"Tonight?" she echoed blankly. "But . . ."

"If your friend still wishes to accompany me she must be ready to leave at midnight. I shall wait for her by the bridge over the Montanka canal. You know it?"

Lucy nodded her head. "Yes but . . ."

"I'm sorry I could not warn you beforehand," Dimitri interrupted. "The boat I am to sail leaves earlier than I had expected. I need to reach the first posting house before dawn. If your friend has changed her mind . . ."

"No . . . no, she will be there!" Lucy was thinking quickly, too dismayed by his news to pay much attention to his faintly apprehensive concentration on the open library door. If she meant to go with him she would have to leave tonight, within the hour almost. Everything was happening so much faster than she had anticipated. There would be no time for her to do more than pack a portmanteau and leave while the ball was still in progress. Fortunate indeed that she had already written her letter for Tante Sophy and grandpère!

"I must go now," Dimitri was saying. "The Fontanka Bridge at midnight!"

When Lucy re-entered the ballroom the musicians had commenced the supper-dance. A glance at her card confirmed her worst suspicions: this dance was promised to Nikolai! As he came to claim her, Lucy wondered if he could possibly read the guilty despair in her eyes, for he gave her a searching look before taking her in his arms and sweeping her onto the floor.

They danced in silence for several seconds, Lucy too engrossed in her own unhappy thoughts to give him her full attention.

"You need not regard me as though I were the greatest monster alive, you know," he remarked, cutting across her thoughts with ruthless precision. "We are to be married—remember? It is expected that we behave in a slightly more familiar fashion than we are doing at present."

Lucy gave him a rather tremulous smile, hoping he would not notice that tears were not very far away.

"Is it?" she asked rather vaguely, concentrating on maintaining her shaky defenses. "In what way?"

"In this way, for one," he replied dryly, tightening his arms about her, and causing her heart to start beating in a most erratic fashion. His head was bent over her own, his lips not very far away from her ear. "It would help if you could contrive to regard me with something at least bordering on affection," he told her.

Thoroughly bemused Lucy glanced up at him. For a moment she could almost deceive herself that the look of melting tenderness in his eyes was really meant for her, and then she remembered the parts they were both supposed to be playing. She bent her head defensively, to conceal her emotions.

"Lucy? Surely I am not such an ogre? Is there something worrying you? Something I can do?"

For a moment she was sorely tempted to tell him; to place her head against the inviting curve of his shoulder and confess everything. However, hard on the heels of that impulse came the knowledge of what his reaction would be. A tremor shook her.

"I assure you there is nothing wrong . . . nothing at all," she said in a tight little voice, she barely recognized as her own, "and if you will please excuse me, I have just remembered something I must do . . ."

"Something more important than taking supper with your new fiancé?" Nikolai asked in an exceedingly dry voice. "Very well, if that is what you wish."

His bow was cold and distant—a stranger's politeness to another stranger, and for a moment Lucy was sorely tempted to call him back and tell him everything. Then reason reasserted itself. She glanced around the ballroom. Grandpère was deep in discussion with another gentleman —Tante Sophy was holding an animated conversation with one of her cronies. With a heart as heavy as lead

183

Lucy left the ballroom, making for her bedroom with dragging feet.

Without Maria's skilled assistance it took longer than Lucy had anticipated to change her gown and find her fur-lined cloak with the result that by the time she had packed a portmanteau, the clock on her dressing table was already pointing to a quarter before twelve.

Silent as a ghost she hurried downstairs, pausing only at the library door to slip inside and place her letter in a prominent position on grandpère's desk. Beside it she put her necklace and Nikolai's ring, in their respective boxes. It had caused her a good deal of heart-searching to give up the ring. She would have dearly loved to keep it as a cherished reminder of her love, but it was no inexpensive trifle, and her aching heart couldn't help thinking that there would be another girl to wear it for Nikolai, and so she left it behind.

The night was exceedingly cold. Without Maria to assist her, Lucy had been compelled to continue wearing her dancing slippers instead of putting on her boots, and she had barely reached Nevsky Prospect before she was shivering convulsively.

The bridge over the Fontanka Canal gleamed eerily under its sugar-coating of frost and Lucy's heart started beating uncomfortably fast when she saw the troika waiting there. Nothing else was in sight; the troika and the horses, dull black smudges against the whiteness of the snow, and the stillness of the frozen canal.

The portmanteau had grown heavier with each step and Lucy was glad to relinquish it to Dimitri. He didn't speak to her, and since she had not yet thought of a convincing reason for having substituted herself for her "friend" Lucy kept her face averted, as he handed her into the troika and wrapped the fur rugs around her. His own face was in the shadows, the collar of his coat turned up against the sharp wind. He made some muffled comment, which she did not catch, and then he was taking his place beside her, the silver traces tinkling slightly as he set the horses in motion.

Clouds obscured the moon and the intense cold had formed a vapour which seemed to hang over the earth as they sped through the night. The horses were as fleet as the wind, with coats the color of ebony. Now that her intentions had been accomplished, she was assailed by numbing despair. Had anyone noticed yet that she was gone? Nikolai perhaps? Her heart gave a traitorous bound and for the life of her she could not prevent herself from peering around the edge of the troika, as though she expected to see her cousin, emerge out of the darkness to carry her home.

St. Petersburg was behind them. Before them lay nothing but frozen stillness, but nothing could compete with the ice that seemed to have invaded her heart.

Lost in her own thoughts, Lucy failed to notice that the horses, obeying her companion's command, were slowing to a halt. When the troika suddenly came to rest by a small grove of silver birches, living up to their name in their winter dress, she stared uncomprehendingly at Dimitri's still figure.

"Why have we stopped?" she queried anxiously.

"Because I thought it time we had a talk," her companion replied evenly, removing his rug, and come to stand beside her, his features clearly exposed for the first time.

"Nikolai! But where is Dimitri? How did you know? What are you doing here?" Lucy gasped, her thoughts in a whirl.

"To answer the last, first, I am here because I wanted to be; and as for young Dimitri, he had the good sense to come to me with your tale about your mysterious 'friend,' who was so anxious to leave St. Petersburg. Oh, don't worry. He has no idea that it was you, but I persuaded him to lend me his assistance in this deception, I have practiced upon you. No need to look at me like that—I promise you he was most unwilling. Now . . . since we are unlikely to be interrupted, let me begin by asking exactly why you found it necessary to flee from me, and in such a very singular manner. Was it perhaps your way of being

185

revenged upon me for Orlov's death? A blow to my pride, which all St. Petersburg could enjoy? Was that it?"

"No . . . how could you think so? It was nothing like that," Lucy cried, appalled by the bitterness in his voice and face.

"Then why?"

The quietly spoken words seemed to fill the silence between them. Fearing that she would be forced into betraying herself Lucy struggled for something to say—any excuse to provide her with a reason for leaving Russia.

"Was it because you still love Orlov?" Nikolai pressed.

Lucy shook her head, unable to lie.

"I never loved Vasili."

"Was it because of this marriage then?"

Betraying tears shimmered in her eyes.

"Was it, Lucy?" His fingers tilted her face toward him.

A small sob shook her.

"Yes!"

The hand that held her face dropped away.

"I see. If I were to promise to release you from it, would you change your mind and stay?"

"How can I? What would Grandpère and Tante Sophy say? They would be so disappointed." To her horror more tears welled in her eyes, rolling down her cheeks.

"Never mind Grandpère and Tante Sophy," Nikolai announced ruthlessly, "and please stop crying, my darling, because if you do not I shall be compelled to use something more effective than words to make you do so. Although I confess to being in scant need of any excuse." He swore softly under his breath, and then Lucy was in his arms, being thoroughly kissed, with an ardor that took her breath away.

Her own lips responded instinctively to Nikolai's urgency, artlessly untutored in their desire to acknowledge and return his passion. Despite the cold, Lucy felt as though her blood was on fire with a warmth that seemed to beat through her body, and then she remembered just what she was betraying! She stiffened automatically, and

186

the next moment, Nikolai lifted his mouth from hers, holding himself in check.

"Don't leave me, Lucy," he muttered huskily. "Like the Princess in your story, your tears have melted my heart, although I own mine was already in a sorry state, long before I saw you cry! Perhaps it would be better if I let you go, for I don't know how I can endure to live in the same house . . . eat at the same table . . . I want you as my wife Lucy, I want you in my arms, as you are already in my heart. When I guessed what you intended to do, I nearly lost my mind. Is marriage to me such an anathema?"

Lucy hid her face against the protection of his coat, too shy now that it had come to the point, to put her love into words.

She felt Nikolai's quickly indrawn breath, breaking the tense silence surrounding them.

"Very well then," he said bitterly. "I shall make arrangements for your departure. You are not to blame because you cannot love me as I love you."

"But I do love you, Nikolai," she whispered shyly. "I think I must have loved you from the first, although . . ."

Her explanations were silenced by the warmth of his mouth, fiercely demanding, as he swept her with him along a fast flowing flood of desire.

The cold darkness faded. There was only Nikolai and the flame of their love, burning higher with every moment that passed.

At last, he put her from him, grasping her hands lightly in his own.

"My foolish little love," he murmured tenderly. "Why did you run away?"

"Because I could not bear to be your wife and not have your love," Lucy admitted shakily.

The look he gave her was so intensely possessive, so indicative of what he felt for her that her heart turned over with tremulous wonder. She would have gone back into his arms, there and then, if she had not had a sudden thought, causing her to frown and bite her lip.

187

"What is it now?" Nikolai asked indulgently. "I trust you have not thought of any other reasons why we should not be married, for I warn you I am in no mood to listen to them!"

Delightful though this assertion was, it served to lighten her frown for only a second.

"Nikolai, I left a letter for Grandpère and Tante Sophy. They will have found it by now!"

He smiled rather wryly and dug into his pocket, producing a small square of paper.

"This note do you mean? I took it from the library and I also took this."

He produced the small box that held her engagement ring, and the next moment had flipped back the lid to reveal the huge sapphire and its attendant diamonds.

"I had this ring made especially for you, my little love, because the sapphire so exactly matches the color of your eyes. Jewels, though, cannot compare with the matchless perfection of those eyes, especially when they are drenched in tears, and those tears are for me. Why couldn't you tell me before?"

"Why couldn't you tell me?" Lucy countered indignantly.

He gave her another rueful smile.

"I could not believe that my love might be returned. We did nothing but quarrel. You made your friendship with Orlov so plain . . . and your disgust for me everytime I came near you . . ."

"Do not remind me!" Lucy cried passionately. "When I think of what I said to you! What I thought! How can you ever forgive me?"

"Oh, I think I shall be able to. When you have paid a suitable price of course. Like one of your sweet kisses for every insult you hurled at me." He saw that she was blushing and laughed.

Lucy had never seen him look so carefree. So young . . . and her heart blazed with grateful joy.

"Tell me you love me," Nikolai commanded unsteadily. "I shall not believe it until I have heard it from your own sweet lips."

Around them the silence seemed to deepen. They were quite alone. The first fine flakes of snow floated gently earthward. The scene had a magical, almost fairy-tale, quality. Lucy remembered the story she had told Nikolai as they travelled to St. Petersburg, and in her smile was all the love she felt for him, all her joy that his heart was not made of ice as she had supposed.

"I love you, Nikolai," she started to say, but the words were crushed against his lips as he took her in his arms, and demonstrated a far more satisfactory manner of exhibiting exactly what her feelings were.

The earth seemed to stand still, and then turn over, so that she did not know whether she was on her head or her heels, and neither did she care, as long as she was held tightly, within the security of Nikolai's protective arms.

Three times he had been there when she needed him the most, and now here he was again; and she was more than willing to pay the forfeit he was demanding of her.

How long they stood together, lost in the wonder of their love, exchanging kisses and murmuring the pledges of newly acknowledged lovers the world over, Lucy did not know, but at last Nikolai gave a rather shaken laugh, and held her away from him, looking down into her eyes.

"Come," he said softly, "we had best get back to our guests. When I took my part in this charade, tonight, I never dreamed it would end so happily. At best I had hoped to persuade you of my own love, and that yours, given time, might grow, but never did I imagine the riches that would be mine. I did not dare to," he added soberly. "At this moment, though, I could almost wish I were Vasili Orlov."

This reference to the man he had thought she loved brought a small frown to Lucy's brow. Was he still not assured that it was *he* who held all of her heart?

"You do not ask why? Nonetheless, I shall tell you. It is because if I were, I should be able to follow the urgings of my heart and carry you off into the night instead of obeying the promptings of reason and rectitude and escorting you back to Tante Sophy, with a whole month to endure before I may properly call you my own.

One last kiss to assure me that I am not dreaming and then we must go, before I forget . . ."

"That you are a gentleman?" Lucy teased gently, as his arms enfolded her and the snow fell gently down upon them as they kissed, lost in the timeless glory of their love.

ABOUT THE AUTHOR
Caroline Courtney

Caroline Courtney was born in India, the youngest daughter of a British Army Colonel stationed there in the troubled years after the First World War. Her first husband, a Royal Air Force pilot, was tragically killed in the closing stages of the Second World War. She later remarried and now lives with her second husband, a retired barrister, in a beautiful 17th century house in Cornwall. They have three children, two sons and a daughter, all of whom are now married, and four grandchildren.

On the rare occasions that Caroline Courtney takes time off from her writing, she enjoys gardening and listening to music, particularly opera. She is also an avid reader of romantic poetry and has an ever-growing collection of poems she has composed herself.

Caroline Courtney is destined to be one of this country's leading romantic novelists. She has written an enormous number of novels over the years—purely for pleasure—and has never before been interested in seeing them reach publication. However, at her family's insistence she has now relented, and Warner Books is proud to be issuing a selection in this uniform edition.